MENDING THE DUKE

A SMITHFIELD MARKET REGENCY ROMANCE
(BOOK 3)

ROSE PEARSON

© Copyright 2018 by Rose Pearson - All rights reserved.

In no way is it legal to reproduce, duplicate, or transmit any part of this document by either electronic means or in printed format. Recording of this publication is strictly prohibited and any storage of this document is not allowed unless with written permission from the publisher. All rights reserved.

Respective author owns all copyrights not held by the publisher.

MENDING THE DUKE

CHAPTER ONE

Lady Alice Parsons alighted from her carriage and was welcomed by her brother and his many staff. She felt greatly relieved that her long journey was finally over.

"My dear brother!" she exclaimed, clasping his hands and looking up into his warm brown eyes, so similar to her own. "It is good to see you again."

"And you." John, the Duke of Royston, smiled back at her with apparent fondness, although there was no spark of joy in his eyes. "Was the journey an arduous one?"

She tried to laugh even though her concern for her dear brother continued to grow by the minute. "It was indeed, as well you know, but you *are* inclined to remain at the furthest estate from town, are you not?"

He shrugged, although she was glad to see the rueful smile on his face. "It was always good enough for Father, so I should think it good enough for me also."

Chuckling, Alice took his arm and greeted the staff, who all appeared to be somewhat relieved at her presence, given the warmth that practically exuded from them all. Alice tried not to let her despair grow, even though all of the worries she had been carrying for so long suddenly burst into life. It was true, then. Her brother was just as distraught as before.

"Have you been *very* busy whilst I have been away?" she asked, as brightly as she could. "I know six months is not particularly long to be apart from one's sister, but I do hope that you have missed me just a little!"

Again, that smile that did not pass to his eyes. "I have been as busy as one is expected to be when one is a Duke," he muttered, passing one hand through his dark, straight hair. "There has been the usual estate business to attend to and, thus far, things appear to be going remarkably well, according to my stewards. I have been relieved to have been excused from all social occasions these last twelve months, although that has recently begun to change."

There was no delight expressed in this, but rather a deep sense of frustration that he, the Duke of Royston, should be requested to come to a dinner or some other event. Alice shook her head to herself, realizing that her brother had still not returned to his former self.

"It is to be expected," she said, as gently as she could. "They are your friends, John, and are only doing what they think is best."

"I do not wish it," he replied, firmly. "I continue to refuse them and have not yet attended a single social occasion. I have no plans to do anything of the sort in the near future."

She arched one eyebrow, looking up at him as he

walked beside her into the drawing room, where tea and refreshments were already waiting. "Even though I have returned?"

That gave him pause, his eyes wrinkling at the corners as he considered what she had said, his square jaw jutting out just a little.

"You may attend whatever you wish," he replied, after a moment. "I shall do no such thing."

Seeing that he was in no mood to discuss the matter further, Alice kept her own counsel and remained silent. The atmosphere grew a little tense, making her stomach churn a trifle uncomfortably as her brother paced up and down in front of the fire. She did not blame him for his behavior, however, for she had very little understanding of what a man in his situation must feel, but she was not, to all intents and purposes, a particularly emotional young lady. Instead, she had more of a practical nature and knew full well that her brother could not simply ignore the fact that he had duties towards both himself and to his friends.

"You are happy to remain here for a time, as you said?"

Glancing up at her brother, she saw that there was something of a darkness in his expression, a deep concern that she was not to remain with him for as long as she had said. Her smile was broad as she nodded, ensuring that he knew there was little to concern him. "But of course, John," she said, practically. "I have no intention of leaving this estate until you require it of me. I am more than content here. After all, it was my home for many years!"

John's relief was evident. "Indeed, it was, and it shall

be as glad as I to have you in residence once more, I am quite sure of it," he replied, with a small smile. "Although I do believe that the manor house Father left you in his will is more than adequate!"

Alice chuckled, her eyes twinkling. "More than adequate indeed, for it even has a gatehouse which I have none other than the gardener residing in since I have no need of it. I have enjoyed being closer to London also. Mrs. Harper, my companion, remains there alone and will be quite relieved to have some time to herself, I am quite sure." Carefully, she poured the tea, before handing him a cup. "Although I should warn you, John, I fully intend to marry by the end of next year. Another Season should do it, I think."

Her brother lifted a brow, regarding her carefully, although he said nothing.

"If what you are asking by that expression is whether or not a few gentlemen have shown any partiality towards me, then I will state that they have! I find them all to be quite decent gentlemen with good character and, of course, a good family."

"Decently titled?"

"Of course." Alice resisted the urge to roll her eyes, knowing that her brother meant well. "I would not think of accepting them were they not."

Grunting quietly, John accepted this and reached for something to eat.

"You will wish to speak to the one I eventually settle on, will you?" Alice murmured, watching John carefully.

There was a short pause. "I suppose I ought to,

although I do not want you to think that I do not trust your judgment, Alice."

That brought a small smile to her face, her heart warming. "Thank you, John. I do appreciate that." She pressed her lips together, considering whether she ought to speak her mind to him but seeing the way he sat back in his chair, now appearing rather tired, she thought it best not to do so. Her words remained unspoken, still lingering on in her mind.

"I should change," she murmured, setting aside her teacup and rising to her feet. "Are we to keep country hours?"

It was as though he did not see nor hear her for a moment, for his gaze took a long time to return to her and even then, she had to wait for a good few seconds before he nodded, slowly.

"Very well, then," she continued, in as bright a voice as she could muster. "A little earlier than I am used to, but it is no great trial! I shall see you at dinner then, John. Do excuse me."

He did not speak to her again, not even so much as to bid her goodbye for the moment, or to assure her that all of her things would have already been set out for her in her bedchamber, as he used to do. There was nothing but silence chasing her away, catching at her heels as she closed the door behind it. Tears sprang to her eyes as she pressed one hand to her mouth, deeply upset at the state of her poor, dear brother.

Slowly, she made her way up the grand staircase and along the hallway, her eyes still damp with tears. Even the old familiarity of the house she had grown up in did not soothe her aching soul. She had very little idea of how she ought to help him, worrying that her presence here would do nothing to pull him from his deep sadness and pain.

Drawing in a deep breath, she stepped into her bedchamber and found that her usual maid, Bessie, was busy putting the last of her things away.

"Do excuse me, my lady!" Bessie exclaimed, scrapping a curtsy. "I did not think –"

"There is nothing the matter, Bessie," Alice replied, with as good a smile as she could muster. "I came up a few minutes earlier than expected. Is my bath drawn?"

Bessie nodded. "Steaming gently, my lady."

A wave of relief crashed over her. "Then I shall go to it at once," she replied, making her way to the dressing room where the bath would be waiting for her. "Thank you, Bessie."

Just as she was about to enter the dressing room, with Bessie following behind her, she paused. Turning, she looked Bessie directly in the eye.

"Has he never recovered?"

Bessie hesitated, her color rising.

"You may speak freely, Bessie," Alice commanded, quietly. "I wish to know the state of my brother and, from what I have seen, I can surmise that he is not in a particularly good frame of mind."

Bessie shook her head, her expression somewhat downcast. "No, my lady. He still mourns his child every day."

Closing her eyes for a moment, Alice fought to regain her composure. It had been almost eighteen months now since John had lost his wife in childbirth, but seeing him today, it was as though he was still at the very beginning of his grief.

"Sometimes, His Grace is up in the nursery, simply staring out at what was meant to be for his child," Bessie continued, a little hesitantly. "I am not certain what it is we should do, my lady, for the staff have been very concerned for him, I can assure you." She shook her head, her lips pulling down. "We were all so very relieved when we learned you were coming back, my lady."

"He does not mourn his wife?"

Bessie blushed furiously, her gaze dropping away again. "I cannot say, my lady. I do not know His Grace's thoughts."

"But he only ever goes to the nursery?" Alice persisted. "He does not go to her bedchamber?"

A look of doubt crept over Alice's features. "His Grace shut the room off, of course, during the year of mourning, but it is now being entirely redecorated, my lady."

Alice drew in a sharp breath, fully aware of what this revealed about her brother.

"But His Grace is truly in such a deep despair that none of us knows how to help him, my lady," Bessie finished, mournfully. "The stewards have been working ever so hard to keep things afloat, and Mrs. Rickert, the housekeeper, has been keeping everything as it ought to be here, of course."

Alice was glad that Bessie had not allowed their difference in station to prevent her from speaking freely about John, for what she had said had given Alice a valuable insight into the life her brother led. She believed every word that Bessie had spoken, more than aware that John had not gone into a marriage of love and affection, but rather one that had been chosen for him before his birth. Lady Penelope Armistice had been of noble breeding and was everything John would want in a wife. She had died only ten months after their marriage, due to complications with the birth of their first child. It had been a terrible, if not common, course of events, but Alice had hoped that her brother would have found a way to have moved on somewhat, especially after the year of mourning that he had completed. Apparently, her hopes had been entirely misplaced.

"I did receive his letters, of course," she murmured, half to herself, recalling the very short notes that had given her nothing but worry. "They always appeared very sad which, of course, I could well understand but I thought that after a year......" She trailed off, her gaze drifting towards the bath that waited for her in the dressing room. With a sad shake of her head, she continued into the room, her mind filled with thoughts about what she might do to help her brother's despondent state of mind.

"Might you consider marrying again, John?"

It was now a good few hours after Alice's bath and she had washed, dressed and had Bessie arrange her hair into a rather sensible chignon, despite the maid's protestations that she could do much better. There was little need to stand on ceremony when one was dining with one's own brother and no other company to speak of!

His glare surprised her. "Do not tell me that you too are to join the many other ladies of my acquaintance who are encouraging me to join the fray once more!" he exclaimed, his hand grasping his glass of wine a little too tightly. "It has only been a year, Alice!"

"Eighteen months," she replied, as gently as she could. "And I can see that you are still rather saddened by the state of it all, John, but I only ask in case it *was* something you had considered so that I might be of assistance to you."

His eyes narrowed a little more. "No, Alice, I do not consider it."

"But you will need an heir," she pointed out, gently. "You are only two and thirty, I know, but as the Duke of Royston, it is important that one begets an heir as soon as possible."

There was a short silence for a moment, and Alice was forced to keep her gaze steady as she looked at her brother, seeing his irritation growing with almost every moment. However, she kept her face calm but her gaze firm, refusing to shy away from the questions.

To her horror, John's eyes suddenly filled, and he turned away, drawing a hand over his eyes for a moment. Her heart broke within her, her breath catching in her throat.

"Oh, John," she began, in a whisper. "I am so terribly sorry. I did not mean –"

"I was to have an heir," he replied, breaking into her thoughts. "I thought I would have a son, I am sure of it.

But he was taken from me, whilst still in his mother's womb. They both left me here alone, Alice."

She swallowed, finding nothing to say that would bring him any kind of comfort.

"You know I did not love my wife," he continued, hoarsely. "But I loved that child, even though it was not yet born. How could I not? It was my own flesh and blood."

Alice wanted to take his hand, wanted to do *something* that would help his anguish but found herself utterly unable to think of a single thing. She had never seen her brother in this frame before, seeing the pain and agony in his eyes as he looked back at her, his face pale and expression wretched.

"I know I will need an heir, Alice, but I cannot bring myself to consider matrimony. Not again. Not now."

"But perhaps –" Her own voice was hoarse and broken, struggling to make clear what it was she was trying to say. "Perhaps a wife would do you good, John. She might bring some joy back to your life."

He shook his head. "Do not speak to me about joy, Alice. It has gone from me for good. I shall not have it in my life again, I fear."

"But you *could*," she persisted, against the growing urge in her mind to cease from talking completely. "I know that things must seem terribly bleak now, John, but you cannot live here alone for the remainder of your days."

He shook his head. "I will not be alone. At least, not for the coming year. You are to remain here with me."

There came no easy answer to him about that. He

was quite right, of course, for she had agreed to remain until the following Season when she might again return to town.

"You will consider it at least, will you not?"

Sighing, he waved a hand. "If I must. But, as you will be here for a good twelve month, I need not think long on it."

To her surprise, he rose from the table, even though dessert had not yet been served. "If you will excuse me, Alice, I am a little tired. I will take port – and whatever other delightful dishes present themselves – in my study."

She had nothing to say, simply watching him go with a heavy heart as she was left alone at the table, aware of the growing darkness seeping into the room. Her brother had walked away with such weariness, as though bearing a terribly heavy weight. How she wished she could take it from him! How she wished she might free him from his shackles, remove him entirely from the dark places in which he walked, where shadows clung to him with every step!

"A twelve month," she murmured to herself, as dessert was set in front of her. "Surely within that time I can find some way to help him?"

She tasted none of the sweetness that burst on her tongue, her mind caught up with the same worries and anxieties over her brother that she had struggled with for so long. All she wanted to do was help him, but what good was that when she had very little idea of what he required? Yes, she was here with him now, but was her presence all that was required for him to recover himself again? She could not believe that it would.

"You will think of something," she said aloud, trying to bolster her own courage. "He will soon be returned to himself. You will see."

But even as she spoke, the heaviness that John carried seemed to drift back to her, blowing out her flickering flame of hope and plunging her heart back into darkness.

CHAPTER TWO

Six Months Later

"I know you must miss them terribly, but you are happy here, aren't you?"

Laura Smith looked down into the miserable face of young Elouise Drover, her heart breaking for the child. At only eight years of age, the young girl had lost both of her parents in one awful moment and had then been sent to the orphanage where Laura worked. Even though Elouise had been with them for a good few months, it was as though she had only been with them a day given the grief that was evident in her face.

"I like the other girls," Elouise admitted, softly, tears dripping onto her cheeks. "But it isn't like home."

An orphan herself, Laura knew full well what Elouise meant and wrapped an arm around the girl's thin shoulders. She remembered the day she had come to the orphanage, with all her earthly possessions wrapped up in a small, threadbare shawl. She had grown up here and now managed to earn a small living by assisting Mary Sanders with the care and protection of the girls. The orphanage was a fairly small building, with a cook and two maids to keep everything in order, and whilst it was nothing compared to the Home for Girls nearby, it certainly wasn't as bad as the poorhouse. There were only thirteen girls altogether, with room for only two more. The girls who came here did not have enough of a fortune to go the Home for Girls, but neither were they so destitute that they were tossed into the poorhouse without a second thought. They were not gentry nor were they the dust of the earth. They still had a hope that they might, one day, find another family and begin life all over again.

For Laura, of course, that hope had never been fulfilled. She had not been adopted, had not so much as been looked at by another family, but at least she had employment and a small income. On top of which, she very much enjoyed encouraging and supporting the girls who came here, knowing exactly what it was they were feeling. That was why she was able to be such a support to Elouise, who was bearing the burden of being left entirely alone in the world.

"You must try to think of it less," Laura explained, as she hugged Elouise. "It will not hurt so much if you let your mind occupy itself with other things."

Elouise sniffed. "What else is there to think about?"

Laura was about to answer when the sound of footsteps reached her ears. Scrambling to her feet, she picked up her basket, turning to see Mary Sanders pushing the door open. Mary was tall and slender, with a practical nature about her that did not often turn into compassion. She was a good fifteen years older than Laura and had come to take over the orphanage at the same time that Laura was looking for employment. Whilst not unfair or cruel, Mary Sanders was not someone who the girls could turn to for comfort or sympathy, for she was a rather unfeeling creature.

"*Do* get on, Laura," Mary said firmly, eyeing Elouise. "You have chores to do and sitting here with a crying child does not help get them done."

Laura nodded. "Yes, I know. Elouise is simply a little distressed and I thought –"

Mary clicked her tongue, interrupting Laura. "No excuses, if you please. Be on your way. Elouise, dry your eyes and then splash some water on your face. I am sure you have something useful you can do. Why not try to continue with your embroidery? It is to be sold once it is completed, remember, so it must be your very best work."

Elouise's lip trembled as she nodded, her brown eyes so filled with pain and grief looking at the floor. Laura felt her heart twist with sympathy for her but, having very little choice but to do what Mary Sanders asked, contented herself with a gentle squeeze of the child's shoulder before stepping past Mary Sanders and making her way to the front door.

Sighing heavily to herself, Laura wished that Mary Sanders could find it within herself to show the girls who came to the orphanage a little more compassion. Instead, it appeared as though she cared nothing for their sufferings, for she always only considered practical arrangements. When a new girl came to the orphanage, Mary was the one to ensure she had a bed, clothing, food and, of course, something to employ herself with which might then be sold and used as income for the orphanage. The orphanage received some funds from their generous benefactors who had opened up the orphanage in the first place, but income from embroidery or other needlework was a welcome addition. Mary Sanders never once thought about grief or sadness or pain when it came to assessing the girls. It was as though emotions did not exist for Mary, as though she did not need to consider them for she had no understanding of them. It was not that way for Laura and, more and more, she found the girls turning to her whenever they needed someone to listen to them. She was glad of that, glad that her experience made her able to understand their difficulties, even if she had Mary Sanders to contend with at times.

Humming to herself, Laura stepped outside into the beautiful afternoon sunshine, tipping her head back for a moment so that she might drink it in. It was by no means warm, given that it was only the beginning of March, but Laura was glad that they had left winter far behind them. The orphanage was always terribly cold in the winter, even with the additional coal they were given. Last winter had been a particularly bad one. She shivered as she stepped out of the gates, making her way towards Smithfield Market where she might collect what they needed for tonight's dinner.

"You ain't cold, Miss Laura, surely?"

Laura smiled at the familiar face of the old market seller, Mr. Stone, standing behind his goods. Tugging her shawl a little closer around herself as the cold wind nipped at her, she shivered again. "I was thinking of the winter," she explained, picking up a couple of potatoes and examining them. "It was a bad one, to be sure. I'm glad the sun has decided to show itself today!"

The old man chuckled, displaying a mouth that was missing a good few teeth. "I can agree with you on that, Miss Laura! Now, what is it you're looking for today?"

Laura picked up yet more potatoes. "Ten of these, Mr. Stone."

"Just ten?"

She chuckled. "Yes, just ten. Cook has more in, you see, so I won't need too many today."

"But you'll be back tomorrow?"

Laughing, she paid him and collected the potatoes in her basket. "I am at Smithfield Market every day, Mr. Stone, as you well know. I'm sure I'll see you again tomorrow."

Mr. Stone's eyes twinkled, and he touched his cap, before letting her move on. Laura, still smiling to herself, continued to walk through the marketplace, making sure she got everything that was needed. Cook wouldn't be best pleased if she came back without!

An hour later, her basket heavily laden, Laura allowed herself to daydream as she made her way back to the orphanage. It was not something she permitted herself to do very regularly, since she felt it was something of a foolish enterprise. She knew her place in this world, knew what was expected of her and what she would, most likely, end up doing for the remainder of her days, but still, she let her thoughts wander. After all, she knew two young ladies from Smithfield Market who had, only recently, had their circumstances change in the most extraordinary of ways. It was foolish for her to believe that she might be next, but still, it showed her that there was always a chance that things might change for her.

She shook her head to herself, berating herself silently. She had no need to think about what *might* happen to her, for that was only filling her with false hope about something that, in all likelihood, would never happen. She would be working at the orphanage for the rest of her days, until she grew too old to do so – or until she had saved up enough money to purchase a small dwelling where she might reside until the last breath left her body. It was by no means a particularly wonderful life, but it was better than so many of the poor and weak around these parts. She could not complain, not when she knew that, had things been different, she might have ended up in the poorhouse or, perhaps, died from consumption. Besides which, the girls needed a listening ear, a gentle heart and quiet reassurance. That was something Mary Sanders lacked, which meant that Laura's role did hold some importance in the running of the orphanage. She did not need to dream about what adventures life could take her on, what gentlemen she might meet or the like. She had to be content with the life she had. Anything else was foolishness.

CHAPTER 2

Walking back towards the gates of the orphanage, Laura stopped dead as her gaze landed on what was the most beautiful carriage she had ever seen. It was practically gleaming in the sunshine, and was surrounded by footmen and tigers who were, clearly, waiting for someone's return. She let her eyes linger on the crest that was emblazoned on the carriage doors, wondering who this might be and why they had come to Smithfield Market.

"Stop your gawking, girl! Be off with you!"

Laura's eyes shot to one of the footmen, who was glaring at her. She drew herself up, refusing to be intimidated. "I am not gawking, sir," she replied, a little tartly. "Simply wondering how I am meant to return to the orphanage when your carriage is directly in front of the gates!"

The footman's eyes narrowed, but he did not rail at her again.

"Might I move past you?" she said, stepping a little closer. "You are all somewhat in the way, I must say."

The footman stepped hastily back, as though she were some disease-ridden creature. "Do be careful, there."

She made her way past him quickly, her back ramrod straight. "Might I ask whose carriage this is?"

"Impertinent chit," the footman muttered, whilst the driver – who appeared much more amicable, shot her a smile.

"The Duke of Royston's sister," he said, sounding rather full of himself. "She has gone into the orphanage, miss. Do you work there?"

"I do," Laura replied, wondering why on earth a Duke's sister had appeared at the orphanage.

The driver grinned, ignoring the footman's disdainful mutterings. "Then you will most likely see her ladyship inside, miss. Lady Alice, or 'my lady', of course."

Laura nodded and smiled, thanking the driver before walking quickly into the orphanage. She did not want to allow herself to hope, but this might mean that the lady was looking to take some girls in! It often happened that the gentry sought out decent maids or the like from places like the orphanage, and Laura was always delighted when it occurred. It was not a particularly wonderful life by any means, but it was more than suitable for girls of the orphanage.

Entering the front door of the house, Laura was met by Helen, a young lady who had only recently begun employment at the orphanage, helping Laura and Mary to deal with the increased number of young girls who had come to the orphanage of late.

"You're wanted in Miss Sanders' office, Laura," she said quickly, taking the basket and shawl from her. "You'd best go at once. There's an awful fine lady in there!"

Laura could not help but smile. "Yes, I saw the carriage. I hope it might mean employment for some of our girls. The gentry are always looking for decent maids and we do have some of the very best trained up here."

Helen looked a little uncertain. "I ain't sure that's who she's looking for, though. She said something about finding 'the perfect girl'. I overheard her as she came in."

Frowning, Laura searched Helen's face, seeing the worry written into her expression. "Even if she provides employment for just one of our girls, then I will be grateful."

"You don't think it's for something a little.....darker?" Helen asked, looking even more concerned. "I have heard of the gentry seeking out a young girl for their own pleasures."

Laura stiffened, then relaxed with an effort. "Mary is not as bad as all that," she said, firmly. "Even if that was the request, I trust that she wouldn't allow such a thing. She has never done so before and I do not think that she would do so now. As much as she may not care for a young girl's emotional state, I can assure you that she *does* consider their future with the greatest of care."

A look of relief passed over Helen's features.

"I had best go," Laura finished, pressing Helen's hand for a moment to take away the last traces of worry. "Thank you, Helen."

Swallowing hard, Laura straightened her skirts, lifted her chin and quickly made her way to towards Mary's office. Whilst what Helen said did have some truth in it – for she herself had heard of gentlemen seeking out young ladies for rather selfish purposes, she did not think that Mary would ever allow such a thing to occur. That would bring down the rather stalwart reputation the orphanage had and, besides which, whilst Mary was very practical and not in the least emotional, Laura had every confidence that she would never send one of her girls to such a terrible future, even if all the money in the world were offered. One thing Mary Sanders had was principles, and she stuck to them without the slightest deviation.

With this in mind, Laura knocked on the door with

confidence, her curiosity growing with every moment as she wondered what this fine lady had come for and, even more so, why she had been requested to attend.

"Enter."

Mary's sharp voice bid her come in and, with a deep breath, Laura opened the door and stepped inside, letting it close softly behind her.

CHAPTER THREE

Alice was rather tired from her long journey back to London but, on seeing the young lady step through the door, felt herself brighten at once. This young lady appeared to be around her own age and had sharp blue eyes that darted to herself and then back towards Miss Sanders. She bobbed a curtsy before Miss Sanders even had the opportunity to introduce them, inclining her head just as she ought.

"My lady, this is Miss Laura Smith, who has employment here at the orphanage," Miss Sanders said, by way of explanation. "Laura, this is Lady Alice, sister to the Duke of Royston."

"My lady," Miss Smith murmured, inclining her head again. "We are honored to have your presence here."

Alice said nothing, quietly thinking to herself just how very well spoken this young lady was.

"She grew up here in the orphanage, before I took over," Miss Sanders continued, gesturing for Miss Smith to sit down. "But since then has taken employment here with the girls. She might be able to advise us a little better as to the matter you have brought to us, my lady."

"And what matter is that?"

Alice was a little surprised at the frankness of this young Miss Smith, seeing her blue eyes filled with something like concern. What did she think Alice was here to suggest?

"I am here in order to find a young girl that will bring joy to my brother's house," she said, clearly. "I thought you might wish to aid and advise me in that, Miss Smith."

Even more astonished at the glare that then came from Miss Smith, Alice blinked rapidly and sat up a little straighter in her chair. Clearly, she had displeased Miss Smith somehow, but had very little idea as to how she had managed to do so.

"May I ask, my lady, what kind of 'joy' your brother is looking for?" Miss Smith asked, her fingers knotting in her lap. "There are young, vulnerable girls here and I do not think that –"

"Ah," Alice interrupted, understanding at once and feeling a sense of horror overtake her. "No, indeed, Miss Smith. You misunderstand me, although I can understand why. I will not be the first member of the gentry to come seeking a young girl for less than honest purposes, I would think."

Miss Smith's jaw clenched whilst Miss Sanders gasped in horror.

"My dear lady, I can only apologize," Miss Sanders exclaimed, shaking one finger at Miss Smith. "Laura, you must express your regret at such a lewd suggestion at once!"

"No, indeed," Alice interrupted again, finding the fact that Miss Smith had asked such a question to be, in fact, rather pleasing. "I am glad that Miss Smith seeks to ensure the good of her girls. It is quite understandable that she should ask something like this, Miss Sanders, given that you only wish the best for the girls in your care. As Miss Smith states, they are already vulnerable."

She turned her gaze onto Miss Sanders, who, looking somewhat nonplussed for a moment, inclined her head again and then turned back to Laura, her eyes still a little narrowed.

"Thank you, my lady," Miss Smith murmured, gently. "I do apologize most sincerely if I have insulted you in any way but, as you say yourself, this would not be the first occasion that gentry have sought out young girls for themselves."

Alice nodded, wondering if this young lady would be amenable to returning to the country with her. She might, she thought, bring a little spark back to the house, back to John's soul.

"May I ask, then, what 'joy' it is that you are seeking for your brother?" Miss Smith continued, her eyes still fixed on Alice's.

Alice held nothing back, choosing to speak frankly with both Miss Sanders and Miss Smith, even though they were by no means her equals. The truth was that she had been struggling with what to do in order to help John heal. After six months of being in his country estate, she had seen him fade into himself all the more, and with the Season fast approaching, she was growing somewhat desperate. Sometimes she had mentioned to John that she would remain at home instead of returning to London for the Season, but he would not hear of it. This was the only idea she had come up with and, with only a few months left until she returned to London herself, she was growing somewhat desperate.

"My brother lost his wife in childbirth some two years ago now," she began, slowly. "It was a very difficult time for him, as you can imagine. Since then, he has been thrown into a deep darkness that he is struggling to escape from. This is not over any sort of love for his late wife, I confess, but rather for the child that died. He has always been rather fond of children, which is somewhat unusual for a Duke, but regardless, I cannot pull him from his misery. I have tried and failed completely. Since I am returning to London for the Season, I thought to come here and seek a young girl to return with me to the estate for a time. Perhaps the joy a child can bring will be all that is required for my brother to finally return to himself."

There was a short silence, where Alice looked from Miss Sanders to Miss Smith and found entirely different expressions on their faces. Miss Sanders appeared delighted, as she had done the moment Alice had greeted her, whereas Miss Smith appeared rather conflicted.

"This child would then remain with you for a few months, before returning to London and to the orphanage?" she said, slowly, her eyes revealing her concern. "That is all?"

Alice felt herself color. "We will, of course, ensure that the child has a good deal of money set aside for her once she returns here, by way of payment, I suppose.

That way, she will have a decent future, at least. And, of course, there will be some recompense towards the orphanage also."

"You are very kind," Miss Sanders said at once, leaning slightly forward in her chair. "I think that we can easily consider your request. Miss Smith, what about Elouise? She is charming, polite and quite quiet."

"Although she is not particularly happy at the moment, Miss Sanders," came the quick reply. "If anything, such an event could brighten her spirits, only to bring them crashing down again when she returns."

Miss Sanders frowned. "Not if she knows her future is secure," she pointed, out quickly. "As Lady Alice has stated, once she returns here she will have the knowledge that, once she reaches her majority, she will be able to live a most comfortable life compared to the rest of the girls here."

From Alice's perspective, this did not appear to bring Miss Smith any consolation.

"I am looking for a child to bring happiness," she reminded them both. "If this Elouise is somewhat distraught at the moment, then I cannot think that –"

"She will be delighted at such an opportunity," Miss Sanders declared, sounding quite sure of herself. "She will be a delight to both you and your brother, I am quite sure of it. Besides which, she comes from a rather better background than most, so will know decent manners and the like."

This made Alice suddenly all the more certain that this young Elouise would fit into the household marvelously. "Wonderful," she said, firmly. "Of course, if the arrangement does not work out, then I shall return the child and ensure that payment is made, as discussed before."

Miss Smith cleared her throat, sitting forward in her chair. "My lady," she began quietly. "I fear that this will do Elouise more harm than good. She will go with you, to a place she has no knowledge of and certainly will be rather afraid at the beginning. She will have no one to turn to, no one to reassure her. Trust is not something that is simply created in a moment, if you will pardon my saying so, which means that she will not turn to you for reassurance. In fact, she will, most likely, turn away from you. Then, should the situation not work out as you hope, she will be sent back more confused and afraid than ever before. Her life has already been thrown into disarray with the loss of her parents and I do not wish to see her so troubled again."

Alice did not lose heart, tipping her head slightly and regarding Miss Smith carefully. It was clear that this young lady cared deeply for the girls in her charge, which she could not fault her for. "Then," she suggested, calmly, "you must attend with her, Miss Smith."

There was a short silence as Miss Smith's eyes flared, clearly astonished at the suggestion.

"Oh, no, my lady," Miss Sanders said, shaking her head. "I cannot allow you that, my lady. I require Miss Smith, you see. She is an integral part of the orphanage here and I cannot do without her."

"Surely there must be someone else you can put in her place for a short few months," Alice said, determined that, even if she had to use her position as the Duke's sister in order to get both Elouise and Miss Smith to attend with her, she would. "After all, I cannot believe that you have these many girls and only one assistant!"

Miss Sanders opened her mouth to speak, only to close it again, as though she were aware she could not simply make an excuse.

"There is Helen," Miss Smith said quietly, although her expression was rather doubtful. "She is fairly new, however, and would require additional training."

Alice smiled, turning to Miss Sanders. "There, you see? There is no need for Miss Smith to remain if you have another young lady you can call on."

Miss Sanders remained entirely silent, turning her sharp gaze onto Miss Smith, who held it steadily.

"It would give Helen more responsibility," Miss Smith said quietly, clearly speaking to Miss Sanders. "And besides which, it would only be for a few months."

Miss Sanders let out a long breath. "It is clear that you are rather interested in going, Laura."

Miss Smith lifted her chin a notch, her eyes sharp. "It is Elouise that concerns me the most, Mary. I will do what I have to in order to ensure her happiness – and the success of Lady Alice's endeavors, of course."

Miss Sanders muttered something under her breath but then, with a heavy sigh, tried to put a smile on her face.

"Well, my lady, if this pleases you, then I shall have both Elouise and Miss Smith ready and prepared for departure later this evening," she said, resigned to the fact that she was not to have her way.

Alice smiled, feeling as though she had finally hit

upon something that might bring her brother out from his doldrums. "Wonderful," she said, firmly. "I am sure that you will both do very well at the Royston estate."

Miss Smith's eyes flickered with interest. "The Royston estate?" she repeated, quietly. "Is that not some distance away?"

Nodding, Alice gave her a small smile. "It is some three days journey, I'm afraid, but it will give us time to talk and get to know one another a little better. I am sure that Elouise will do wonderfully and be very excited about the trip."

Miss Smith, however, did not look as convinced as Alice felt but, at the very least, appeared to be quite content with the situation as it now stood.

"You are very kind to think of us, Lady Alice," Miss Sanders murmured, with a small smile. "Miss Smith, you should go and prepare Elouise for what is to come. You must be ready to depart by five o'clock."

"Of course."

Miss Smith rose to her feet, turned towards Alice and gave another curtsy, a small smile on her face. "Until this evening, Lady Alice. And thank you."

"No," Alice murmured, as Miss Smith left the room. "Thank you, Miss Smith."

CHAPTER FOUR

Some three days later and Laura found herself wishing that the journey to the Royston Estate would come to a close. It was not that she was in any way homesick, or that she was eager to return to London, but rather that the somewhat cramped quarters of the carriage – as luxurious as it was – meant that she had very little room to move. The two overnight residences had been lovely, however, and even she had to admit that to be waited on in such an unusual manner was quite wonderful. She had not had to ask for anything, for every single thing that she would require had been presented to her. New gowns were brought for both herself and Elouise to change into on the final day of their travel, having been purchased by Lady Alice in London before they had quit the town. Lady Alice, in her kindness, had promised that they should both have a new wardrobe waiting for them once they had arrived at the estate.

Thankfully, Elouise had been pulled from her own

misery by news that she was to have a short holiday in a Duke's home and had become a whirlwind of giddy excitement the moment Laura had explained to her what was to occur. Almost everything seemed to add to her anticipation of reaching the estate, although Laura was always sure to warn her not to become used to such luxuries as they were currently receiving. She was, however, very glad to see the girl so delighted and happy, seeing a light in her eyes that had not been there before. Perhaps Miss Sanders had been correct in putting Elouise forward after all.

She herself had been rather unsure about it all, although the moment Lady Alice had suggested it, she had found herself caught up with the idea almost at once. It had been difficult to leave the orphanage and the girls behind, but the fact that Helen took her place brought her a good deal of relief. Helen was kind and gentle and would take very good care of the girls in her charge. She would protect them from Miss Sander's abrasive nature. It was going to be a very unusual experience, residing in the Duke's estate, and Laura allowed herself a little excitement at the thought. It would be an adventure, she was quite sure! She just hoped that Elouise's presence would be able to bring the joy that Lady Alice felt was so necessary for her brother's restoration.

In the back of her mind, Laura could not help but wonder what the Duke of Royston, might look like. From Lady Alice's description, she thought he would have something of a dark, almost foreboding appearance, as though everything in this world brought him nothing but anger and frustration. He was, at least, a good and kind man, according to Lady Alice's description, which meant that she was not at all fearful for either herself or Elouise's safety. That was a relief, at least.

Lady Alice was a very warm-hearted young lady who clearly cared a good deal for her brother. Laura felt as though they had known one another for much longer than they had, given that they were able to converse easily about a good many things. It was not usual for such a refined lady to even converse with such lowly person as Laura knew herself to be but, then again, this was something of an unusual situation. Lady Alice had spoken more about her brother during their journey to his estate and Laura had felt herself grow with sympathy for both him and Lady Alice herself. It sounded as though His Grace had lost more than just his child and wife, but that he had lost something of himself in the midst of it all.

"Now, here we are!"

Lady Alice's voice was somewhat shrill, betraying her relief at returning to the estate. Elouise, who had been chattering excitedly with both Lady Alice and Laura, now fell silent, her face almost pressed against the window of the carriage as she looked out. Laura allowed her to do so without reprimanding her, seeing the small smile on Lady Alice's face as she watched Elouise.

"My goodness," she murmured, as the estate came into view. "It is truly magnificent, Lady Alice."

The manor house was bigger than anything Laura had ever seen. Its many windows, too many to count, shone in the sunshine, sparkling as they caught the light. The gardens were vast, spread out like a green carpet ahead of them, just waiting to be explored by an inquisitive child such as Elouise.

"It is a castle!" Elouise exclaimed, in a whisper. "A very, very big castle."

Lady Alice chuckled. "I can see why you might think so, my dear, although it does not have the turrets that one would expect of a castle."

Laura smiled as Lady Alice patted Elouise fondly on the shoulder, clearly quite taken with her already.

"And I am really to stay here?" Elouise asked, turning her face back to Lady Alice for a moment, her eyes wide with wonder.

Again, Lady Alice laughed softly, her eyes delighted. "Of course, you are, my dear girl. You are already bringing me a good deal of happiness and I am quite sure that we will all be the better for having both you and Miss Smith here."

"I do hope so," Laura murmured aloud, catching Lady Alice's eye. "Might I ask, Lady Alice, does the Duke know of your plan?"

Lady Alice hesitated for a moment, the light in her eyes fading. "No, he does not," she said, slowly. "I will not pretend that he will be truly delighted with your presence here, Miss Smith, but I hope that in time, he will come to enjoy it."

Laura nodded slowly, her eyes drifting towards Elouise who was still making all manner of exclamations.

"I will ensure that nothing cruel is said to Elouise, of course," Lady Alice said firmly, as though she recognized Laura's thoughts. "If he does not greet you warmly, however, do not allow it to torture your thoughts. He is, as I have said, in something of a dark place."

Trying not to allow her sudden anxiety to fill her heart, Laura attempted to smile. "But of course," she said, quickly. "I quite understand. Elouise will be overcome by it all, I am sure, and will most likely not notice a thing."

There was no more time to say anything for the carriage now arrived at the top of the long drive, with a few footmen scrambling down the steps towards the carriage, ready to help her alight.

"My goodness," Laura breathed, as the footman took her hand and helped her out of the carriage, her eyes caught by the magnificence of the manor house. "This is truly wonderful, Lady Alice."

She smiled. "I am glad you think so. And what say you, Elouise? Do you think you will be happy to reside here with me for a time?"

Elouise had gone rather white, although a dazzling smile remained on her face. A little concerned that the child was to faint, having been overcome by the sight and sound of everything so wonderful, Laura put an arm around her shoulders.

"Thank you, Lady Alice," Elouise whispered, her voice rather hoarse. "Yes, I will be very happy to stay here with you."

"Alice? Is that you?"

Laura caught her breath as the voice of a gentleman reached her ears. He was striding towards them all, a tall, broad figure with dark eyes that lingered on her for a moment, sending flurries of anxiety into her belly.

"Ah, John," Lady Alice said, putting a broad smile on

her face as she turned towards her brother. "I do hope you have not been too melancholy whilst I have been away."

He frowned, not even a hint of a smile on his face. "No," he said, shortly. "I have had plenty to keep me occupied."

"Very good," Lady Alice said, with a warm smile. "May I present Miss Smith and her charge, Miss Elouise Drover."

Laura kept her head up, her eyes fixed, as she looked into the Duke's face, finding him to be a most intimidating creature. He was looking back at her with flat, brown eyes that held not even the faintest spark of light. His jaw was set, his thick eyebrows furrowed into a deep frown as he regarded her. She felt as though he was looking into her very soul, sending shudders all through her.

"Why are they here?"

His voice was low and grating, his expression nothing other than sheer disdain.

Lady Alice cleared her throat. "They are here as my guests."

"And where did they come from?" the Duke asked, clearly angered with his sister. "I did not think that you passed the time with people of such a rank."

Laura felt herself bristle at the Duke's unkindness, keeping her arm around Elouise's shoulders. Could the Duke not see that his sister was doing what she could to help him? Did he not look at Elouise and see that she was hanging on to his every word and could easily understand the disrespect coming from his mouth?

"I have chosen to take in Elouise for a time, John," Lady Alice said clearly, her voice a little stern. "Miss Smith is here to ensure that she does as is expected, that is all."

"And when do they return?"

Lady Alice paused and, from where she stood, Laura could see that she had curled one of her hands into a small fist. It was clear that she was frustrated with the Duke's reaction, even though she had already warned Laura that he might behave in such a way.

"They will return with me when I go back to London for the Season," she said, firmly. "Does that please you?"

"I am glad to make your acquaintance, your grace."

Laura stepped forward, looking up at the Duke calmly as he let his eyes rest on hers again. She could see the way his eyes flickered, the way his lips tugged into a thin, tight line. He did not even consider answering her, for he turned on his heel and walked back into the house almost the moment he had finished speaking.

"Oh, dear," Lady Alice sighed, shaking her head. "I did hope that he....."

"You have nothing to apologize for, Lady Alice," Laura said quickly, not wanting the lady to take on any kind of guilt. "You did warn me that the Duke might be less than pleased with our presence and it appears you were quite right."

Lady Alice sighed again, her eyes filled with moisture. "You do not know how difficult it has been, Miss Smith. My brother has become a little more lost with every day that has passed, to the point that I have been quite unable to help him. I do not know what it is I ought to do. I did hope that even the sight of Elouise might bring a smile to his face but now he appears to be rather angry with me." She shook her head again, pulling out a lace handkerchief and dabbing at her eyes. "I have very little idea of what else there is for me to do, Miss Smith, and so it seems we must persevere. Perhaps, in a few days' time, he will be less inclined to turn away from you both without a word. In fact, I insist that you join us for dinner, although I suspect it will be a little late for Elouise. Regardless, she is to have the run of the house, aside from my brother's quarters and his study. Her presence here should be felt, you understand. She is not to be hidden away."

"I quite understand," Laura replied, wishing she could bring Lady Alice a little more comfort. "You can trust me to do as you wish, my lady. I am sure that, in time, the Duke will be glad of what you have done for him. It is obvious that you care about him very much."

There appeared a small smile on Lady Alice's face, replacing the morose sadness that had been etched there only moments before. "Thank you, Miss Smith. You have been a wonderful companion thus far and, in fact, I have found my worries growing somewhat less whenever I speak to you. Even now, you have reassured me that my brother's attitude will improve."

Laura smiled, glad that she had been able to do so. "Of course, my lady," she murmured, inclining her head.

"Are we to go inside now?"

Laura's smile spread as she looked down at Elouise, who was clearly not put off by the Duke's words in the least. Instead, she was still looking rather excited, her hand reaching for Laura's as her eyes lingered on Lady Alice, a shy smile on her face.

"Of course, you must come inside," Lady Alice exclaimed, laughing. "You have been waiting out here for much too long already. Thank you for your patience, Elouise."

Elouise's fingers tightened on Laura's as she climbed the stone steps that led to the manor house, and Laura felt a swirl of excitement catch her by surprise. Despite the Duke's unwelcoming manner, despite Lady Alice's fears, Laura realized she was truly looking forward to her time at the Royston estate. It was more than she had ever allowed herself to dream of, being nothing more than a lowly young lady employed in the orphanage, and yet here she was, stepping into the biggest house she had ever seen.

"You have your own bedchamber next to one another, of course," Lady Alice said, guiding them towards the staircase. "And there should be a bath drawn for each of you. A maid will attend you, Miss Smith, and there shall be another for you, Elouise." She smiled as Elouise gasped in astonishment. "Then there shall be dinner for you, Elouise, with the maid assigned to you and with the company of Miss Smith also. Miss Smith, if you would care to join myself and the Duke for dinner, then I would be most glad of your company. There will be time for adequate preparation, of course, and the wardrobe in your bedchamber has all the necessary gowns and the like." She waved a hand, as though this was all something Laura should have expected, as Elouise began to tug Laura up the stairs.

"Until this evening then, Miss Smith," Lady Alice called, as they followed a maid up the stairs who was to show them to their rooms. "I am already looking forward to it."

"As am I," Laura replied, with as much honesty as she could muster.

CHAPTER FIVE

"*E*louise?"

Laura pushed open the bedchamber door to find Elouise still eating breakfast, her face lighting up when she saw Laura.

"Come in!" Elouise squeaked, trying to swallow her toast. "I slept a little later than I ought, Miss Smith, but the maid did not seem to mind."

Laura smiled and sat down opposite her charge. "Of course. You are allowed to sleep for as long as you wish here, although I need not remind you that –"

"I shouldn't become used to it," Elouise said firmly, with a small shake of her head. "Yes, Miss Smith. So you have said on a number of occasions."

Stifling her laugh, Laura kept her gaze steady. "That is because it is easy to become used to these luxuries," she said, firmly. "I will admit that it's wonderful to have breakfast brought to you, to enjoy all the wonderful delicacies that we have eaten lately, but we must remember where we have come from and where we are going back to."

Elouise's eyes dimmed for a moment. "I know," she said, quietly. "I am not forgetting, Miss Smith."

"Although," Laura continued, as Elouise drank the last of her tea. "I do not think that you will need to worry about what you will do with the rest of your life, my dear. Did Miss Sanders tell you what Lady Alice will do for you?"

Elouise shook her head mutely, her eyes a little wide.

"Well," Laura said, feeling a warmth clutch at her heart. "She is to give you a small sum of money on which you will be able to live on for the rest of your life, if you are careful." She smiled as Elouise gasped, her eyes widening all the more. "You will not need to consider your future in the same way as the other girls do."

There came, then a few minutes of nothing but silence, broken only by the crackling of the fire in the grate. Laura let Elouise consider what she had been told in silence, her lips still curved in a gentle smile.

"Lady Alice is very kind," Elouise said, after a while. "Very kind indeed, don't you think?

"Yes, she is very generous," Laura agreed, having nothing but respect for the lady.

"But the Duke himself does not care for us," Elouise continued, in a practical voice. "I don't think that he likes us being here very much at all."

Laura wanted to shake her head and tell Elouise that she was wrong, that the Duke was simply a quiet man who kept himself to himself, but the words wouldn't come. She couldn't tell Elouise an untruth.

"The Duke is quiet and can appear very irritable, yes, but I cannot tell what he really thinks of us being here," she said slowly, admitting to her charge that the Duke did appear to be rather frustrated with their presence. "Lady Alice thinks that it will be for his good for us to remain here and so here we must remain. After all, it has only been a few days that we have been here thus far, and we have a few more months ahead of us at least! Just think what changes might come over the Duke in that time. I am sure that he will accept us both very soon."

Elouise did not look convinced but neither did she look particularly upset. Instead, she simply shrugged and took another bite of toast.

"Shall I leave you to eat and then dress?" Laura asked, with a slightly wry smile. "You are nowhere near finished and I'm sitting here doing nothing but talking to you!"

Elouise grinned. "Should you like to play hide and go seek today, Miss Smith?"

That had Laura pausing for a moment. "Hide and go seek?"

"Yes," Elouise said, fervently. "This is such a wonderfully big house that I have been longing to play it ever since we arrived."

It was on the tip of Laura's tongue to say no, to tell Elouise that such a game would not be wise in the Duke's estate, only for the words Lady Alice had said on arrival to come back to her mind.

She is to have the run of the house. Her presence should be felt. She should not be hidden away.

"Well, I suppose we might," she said slowly, aware of

just how delighted Elouise appeared. "We are not to go near the Duke's bedchamber or his study – in fact, not even his library, Elouise. If you choose to hide anywhere near there, then the game must be at an end."

Elouise nodded solemnly. "Of course, Miss Smith. I understand."

"Good." Getting to her feet, Laura chuckled as Elouise began to eat her toast a little more quickly. "Then I shall go and hide somewhere near to the drawing room, Elouise, and once you are dressed and ready, you can come in search of me. I shall make the sound of a mouse if you are struggling to find me so ensure that you are listening carefully!"

"Oh, I shall!" Elouise exclaimed, her eyes shining. "I shall not be long, Miss Smith!"

Still laughing softly to herself, Laura left the room, her face wreathed in smiles. The Duke's despondent mood and the clear disdain he had for both herself and Elouise did not appear to be affecting her charge in any way at all. Therefore, she would not allow it to affect her mood either.

Hurrying down towards the drawing room, Laura could not help but reflect on the Duke of Royston. He had not always come to join herself, Lady Alice and occasionally Elouise to dine these last few days, which Lady Alice had said was not particularly unusual. She had often had to dine alone, she had said, which had made Laura feel even more sorry for her. The Duke, however, she felt less compassion for, given that he demanded silence from both herself and Elouise whenever he came to sit, which both she and Elouise steadfastly ignored.

CHAPTER 5

They continued their conversations despite his barked demands for silence, as did Lady Alice which was something of a relief. She was struggling to see how he was truly such a poor, unfortunate soul when all she could see from him was nothing more than anger and selfishness.

Sometimes, she caught herself wondering what he might look like if he smiled. Thus far, he had not smiled at her on a single occasion, nor had he even smiled at his sister. Laura was quietly convinced that it would change his entire demeanor, having never seen him do anything other than frown or glower at her. There was something curious about him, even though she was rather frustrated with his continual dismissal of Elouise in particular. She found that she could understand Lady Alice's urge to help him, not that she herself felt in any way capable of offering any kind of suggestion.

Soon, however, she was tugged from her thoughts by the sound of Elouise's hurried feet coming down the staircase, her giggles already echoing around the manor house. Having not yet found a single place to hide, Laura looked about frantically, before stepping behind a rather large clock, hoping Elouise would not immediately spot her.

What soon followed was a jolly good game of 'hide and go-seek'. Elouise was true to her word and did not go near the Duke's library, nor his study nor did she climb the staircase, for fear it would take her much too close to the Duke's quarters. Laura found herself vastly enjoying the game, taking almost as much delight in it as Elouise herself. At one point, Lady Alice stopped by, her eyes bright as Elouise bid her to hush so that Laura would not find her. But find her she did, and soon the three ladies were laughing together.

"I am so very glad that you are doing just what I suggested," Lady Alice murmured, as she carefully pulled on her riding gloves. "No hiding this young lady away. John – the Duke – needs to be forcibly pulled from his mire, I fear."

Laura gave her a small smile, knowing what she meant, only for Lady Alice to excuse herself and step away, saying that she intended to enjoy the good weather by taking a ride. Laura bid her farewell, as did Elouise, before she went to hide yet again, even though it was Laura's turn.

"You are cheating, Elouise!" Laura laughed, her hands planted firmly on her hips as she looked all around her. "You know very well it is my turn to hide."

"Will you *please* stop that infernal racket!"

Twisting her head about and feeling her stomach drop to her toes, Laura saw that none other than the Duke was approaching them, his stance practically rigid as he drew closer to them.

"I have had more than enough of this noise, Miss Smith!" he exclaimed, his eyes almost wild with fury. "I have been trying my best to dine in peace but all I hear is yourself and that child making as much noise as you possibly can!"

"Really, your grace, you are exaggerating," Laura replied firmly, stopping him dead in his tracks. "And I will not have it, I confess." She kept her gaze steady, looking up at him and steadfastly refusing to be intimidated. Lady Alice had said that Elouise was to be treated as a guest of hers and that was precisely what she was doing.

He snorted. "Exaggerating? The whole house was shaking with the shock of your heavy footfalls. This is not a nursery, Miss Smith, and I would ask you not to treat it as such."

She did not turn from him. "Your sister has made it abundantly clear that Elouise is not to be hidden away, your Grace. I am simply doing what she asked."

His eyes narrowed. "My sister is not lord of this estate!"

Laura did not say anything, simply looking up at him as calmly as she could, glad that Elouise was, most likely somewhere where she could not hear the Duke speak. "And yet she has a more generous heart than you, it appears."

For a long moment, he did not speak. Instead, he stared at her as though he was not quite sure what to do with her, as though astonished that anyone should have the audacity to speak to him as such.

"The noise is quite disturbing," he said curtly, after a moment. "That is all I have to say on the matter."

"It is merely laughter," she replied quickly, not allowing him to turn away. "A child ought to be allowed to laugh, your grace. It seems to me that there is not enough of that within these four walls."

That appeared to make him even angrier than he had been before. Spots of color appeared on his cheeks, his eyes flashed, and he held himself ramrod straight.

"You ought to learn some manners, Miss Smith,

although mayhap that is too much to ask of a young lady from your lowly background!"

His words stung, and she shrank back, as though he had slapped her. Almost at once, his demeanor changed, as though he had realized what he had said. His eyes lost their fire, his gaze dropped to the floor and the tension left his shoulders.

Laura tried her best to keep her breath steady, growing angrier with him by the minute despite the shame that sent a flush to her cheeks. This Duke was attempting to mortify her simply because she came from a different sort than he.

"I would have thought that generosity and understanding might have pervaded the hearts of the nobility towards those less fortunate than themselves," she whispered, her lips shaking as she spoke, "but it appears not to be so. I cannot help that both my parents were taken from me, in the same way that Elouise cannot help that she was left here on this earth alone. We are grateful for small mercies, your grace, and even more grateful to your sister for her kindness. This is something that Elouise has never before experienced and, most likely, will never experience again. It does not appear to me that it is either myself or Elouise that needs to learn manners or the like, your grace, but rather that there is more for *you* to learn about how one ought to treat others, particularly those who have no sisters or brothers or any kind of family to speak of." She hated that tears had crept into her eyes, choosing not to blink them away but to let them fall to her cheeks if they chose to. "If you will excuse me, your grace,

I need to continue my game with Elouise. She is waiting for me."

She turned and walked away from him, not caring whether or not he had anything else to say to her. She could feel his glare boring into her spine but kept herself from turning back to glance at him, walking into the drawing room to find Elouise standing in the middle of the room.

Her eyes were round saucers, her cheeks deathly pale and, for a moment, Laura was worried that the child was about to faint. She made to rush over to her, only for Elouise to blink rapidly, some color coming back into her cheeks.

"Are you quite all right, my dear?" Laura asked, a little breathlessly. "I do apologize, I was just coming to find you when –"

"You were speaking to the Duke."

A slow frown crept over Laura's expression. "I was."

"And he was angry with us."

"He was," Laura agreed. "But he had no need to be and I was not afraid to tell him so, my dear. Lady Alice has said that we can play wherever we wish in the house so you don't need to worry."

Elouise's lips trembled. "Are you sure?"

Laura smiled, pushing her anger and irritation at the Duke's callousness aside. "I am quite sure," she said, firmly. "Now, shall we continue to play or would you like to go for a walk in the garden for a while? We might be able to play 'hide and go-seek' there too, if you wanted."

Thankfully, Elouise brightened, her smile chasing away her anxiety. "Yes, I would like that," she exclaimed, heading back towards the door. "I will need my hat and my gloves though, I think, since it is a little cold."

Laura made to say that the maid would be able to fetch those things for her, but then chose not to say anything at all. It was good for Elouise to go and fetch those things herself, so that she wouldn't get too used to having someone else fetching everything she needed. Slowly, she followed after her, a small smile on her face as a sense of satisfaction filled her. She had no regrets about speaking to the Duke in the way she had done, for he was being rather cruel and intolerant towards Elouise which flew in the face of Lady Alice's kindness. She did not see the Duke standing in the shadows, his eyes lingering on her as she walked away, a look of confusion etched across his face.

CHAPTER SIX

*J*ohn was angry.

He did not like what his sister had done in bringing this girl and her companion with her to the house. He did not like that Alice, even in her good will, had done such a thing without so much as asking him what he thought of it all. Instead, she had simply done it without so much as a thought as to what he would say and thus he had found his life completely altered by the presence of two unwanted guests.

And yet, there was something about Miss Smith that brought him nothing but confusion. The way she spoke to him, the calm, unhindered way she looked up at him and said everything that was going on in her heart, gave him pause. She was not like any other lady of his acquaintance, bar his sister, for they all fawned all over him. They had done ever since he had first gone to town for the Season, for he knew that the aim of most mothers of the *ton* was to marry their daughters to as good a title as they could. That had done nothing for him, of course, given that his marriage had already been arranged, and he found that he had grown rather weary of their constant attentions and flattery.

But this was not the case with Miss Smith. She was more direct than anyone he had met before, speaking to him in a clear, firm voice and not so much as flinching when he railed at her. The way she'd spoken to him had shown him her frustration and upset, which had brought a small stab of guilt to his heart. It meant very little to him, of course, for he was quite sure that he was in the right when it came to demanding peace in his own home, but he could not forget the way her eyes had filled with unshed tears as she'd gazed up at him, even though it had been two days since the event. He had remained in his own quarters since then, choosing not to dine with his sister and Miss Smith, telling himself that it was simply because he preferred his own company and not because he did not want to face Miss Smith again.

Closing his eyes, John leaned his head back against the overstuffed chair and tried to put Miss Smith from his mind but found that he could not. Even now, her words resounded with him and he could not rid them from himself. They lingered on, sending barbs of guilt and shame into his heart – feelings he had not experienced in some time.

"What am I to do about her?" he muttered to himself, passing one hand over his eyes. "She is infuriating."

Infuriating and intriguing.

In his heart, John knew that Miss Smith had been correct to rail at him, even if he did not want to admit it. He had been overly harsh with Elouise, for the sound of her laughter had not irritated him as he'd suggested but had brought a spark of happiness back into his soul.

He did not want to feel any such emotion. He was much too used to the safety and security of sadness and loneliness that surrounded him with every passing day, for he knew he made no effort to battle them at all. Whilst he had much appreciated Alice's company of late, he had found that there had been no increase in his joy. This was, most likely, because whilst he found her company pleasing, he also knew that she was worried about him. There was always something underlying whenever they were together, something nervous, something anxious, something that unsettled him even more than he already was. He was still trapped with the pain of losing his unborn child, still struggling with the loss of the happiness he had expected to have. And yet, in the midst of it all, he had refused to allow himself to feel the joy at having the laughter of a child echoing through the house. It was as if it was too much for him to bear and so he had turned towards anger, growing frustrated with Miss Smith and Elouise when he had very little need to do so.

"I shall have to apologize to her," he muttered to himself, even though everything in him rebelled at the idea. "Even it is that I just say that I ought not to have been so gruff."

Perhaps that would be enough to remove the lady from his thoughts. Muttering darkly to himself, John pushed the chair back and stood up, straightening his cravat carefully before quitting the room.

. . .

As he walked into the library, he was astonished to find his sister Alice reading aloud to Elouise. In fact, he was so taken with the scene that he was forced to stand completely still, feeling as though all of the air had been dragged from his lungs. Alice was reading aloud from a children's book and Elouise was snuggled in next to her, her head resting on Alice's shoulder. It was a picture of happiness and contentment and, as he watched, John felt something in his heart wrench. This was what he had hoped for in his own life and it had been taken from him. Of course, Alice had tried to convince him that he could have such a thing again – and well he could, of course, if he tried to find himself another wife, but there was something in him that held him back from doing so. He did not want to have to go to London, to parade himself through all the many social occasions that the *ton* would throw during the Season only to have a good many milk-water misses bat their eyes at him with nothing but an insipid character and beautiful face to show for themselves. But yet, even still, he longed for a wife and family of his own. That desire had never left him.

I do not want a wife who will be just the same as my first wife, he thought to himself, dragging his eyes away from his sister and Elouise in search of Miss Smith. *I want someone who genuinely cares for me instead of seeing me as just my title and fortune.*

It was a ridiculous notion, of course, particularly for a Duke but the hope that such a thing might, one day, occur did not instantly leave him. Instead, he let it linger, his eyes falling on Miss Smith as she sat reading quietly in the corner, clearly unaware of his presence.

CHAPTER 6

Clearing his throat, John walked towards her, hearing Alice pause in her reading for a moment, only to resume it again. Glad that his sister and Miss Elouise would be distracted for a moment, for he did not want to be overheard, John gave Miss Smith a small smile as she looked up at him, clearly a little surprised to see him.

"Your grace," she murmured, looking to get up from her seat, but John waved her back.

"There is no need to rise," he said, one hand on the back of the chair opposite her. "Might I sit with you for a moment, Miss Smith?"

Her eyes rounded but she nodded and he sat down gratefully, hoping that she was not afraid of him in any way.

"Miss Smith," he began, clearing his throat again as the words stuck in his throat. "I.... Miss Smith, I think I should begin by apologizing to you for some of the things I said to you in our recent meeting."

She tipped her head a little to the side and he saw, for the first time, just how vividly blue her eyes were. "Oh?"

Hesitating for a moment, John took a breath to collect his thoughts before continuing on. "Indeed. I was very rude to you, Miss Smith, and for that, I apologize. I was angry and frustrated and should not have allowed such emotions to become evident in my speech."

There was a moment of silence.

"Yes," Miss Smith said after a moment. "Yes, you were very rude, your grace."

A flush of heat crept up his neck and into his face, growing aware that, yet again, Miss Smith was speaking to him like no other person would. "For that, I apologize, as I said, Miss Smith."

She considered him for another moment. "Elouise was rather upset, your grace. I had to speak to her calmly and patiently, to reassure her that it was nothing she herself had done that had made you rail at me in such a loud fashion. She heard every word, I'm afraid, and it has taken a good deal of convincing from both myself and Lady Alice before she would set foot in the drawing room or the library again."

He nodded, his shame growing by the moment. "I would be quite glad to show Elouise that she is most welcome here, Miss Smith, if that would settle your mind."

A small smile settled on her lips and, to his astonishment, John found himself smiling back at her.

"That would be most welcome, I am sure, your grace," she said, carefully. "Although might I suggest that you do not disturb her at this present moment, for she is heartily enjoying a story with Lady Alice, as you can see."

A question stuck in his throat, trying its best to be spoken aloud but John found that he could not bring himself to do so.

"She is doing wonderfully well," Miss Smith continued, softly. "I am truly glad for her. She was so very miserable."

"And –" John began, the words tumbling out of his mouth now. "If I make reparations with Miss Elouise, might you then consider forgiving me for my unpardonable rudeness towards you?"

Her smile stretched across her face and relief flooded

him. "But of course, your grace. It would not do for a lady of such a lowly background as myself to withhold pardon from someone such as yourself!"

A flush caught his cheeks. "I would not have you do so without being willing, Miss Smith."

"But willing I am," she replied, gently. "Have no fear, your grace. I have received a good many insults in my life thus far and most of them have been a good deal worse than what you said."

That did nothing to please him but rather sent his soul into a flurry of concern. "Is that so?" he asked, realizing that he knew nothing about this young lady. "Might I ask if you too come from the same background as Elouise, then? You may have told me before, I understand, but I have not always paid a good deal of attention."

At his blush of shame, Miss Smith laughed gently and smiled at him, her blue eyes now sparkling with warmth instead of being icy with cold. "I do not mind saying so again, your grace. Yes, I too am without family, for both my parents died when I was young. I spent my life in the orphanage at Smithfield Market in London and it is from there that I come here. I managed to secure employment at the orphanage when Mary Sanders agreed to keep me on." Her lips twitched. "We do make a good pair, I confess, for Mary Sanders is of a much more practical sort than I. It is quite understandable, I suppose, since she has never had to endure the difficulties that come with being an orphan."

This made him pause. "By this," he said slowly, thinking hard, "you must mean that Mary Sanders does not often see the tears in the eyes of those that come to you?"

She nodded, her eyes growing a little sorrowful for a moment. "That is quite correct, your grace. I think that both are of equal importance when it comes to ensuring that a girl is as happy as she can be in a very trying situation."

"And what of me?"

The words slipped from his mouth before he could restrain them. Miss Smith looked surprised.

"What I mean is," he said, floundering just a little. "Do you think, as my sister clearly does, that having Elouise present will help my emotional state, as dire as it is?" He felt very strange, opening himself up in such a vulnerable fashion with a lady he did not know particularly well at all, but there was something about her that made him want to do so and, to his relief, she did not seem to find his question in any way ridiculous.

"I do hope so, your grace," she said, quietly, her eyes betraying her growing compassion for him. "I cannot imagine what you have endured. It must be a deep, unflinching agony, I expect. An agony which you cannot truly explain to anyone."

His throat grew a little tight as she continued to speak, wondering how she was able to see into his very soul.

"I have seen such a pain in many a girl's eyes," she continued, softly. "And there are a good many things that can bring some relief, but I would state that these things differ for each person. One cannot tell you that what worked for them will, therefore, be sure to pull you from your misery, but I would think it wise to give each thing a try before discarding it."

John glanced towards Elouise, hearing her laugh as Alice read something funny on the page in front of her.

"I suppose you are correct, Miss Smith," he said, getting to his feet. "You have given me much to consider." His eyes fell on the book she had been reading, his eyes rounding as astonishment filled him.

"You are reading a book on chess?"

She looked up at him, her brows furrowed. "I may be from the streets of London, my lord, but I can read. In fact, I enjoy reading very much and have done as much as I can these last years."

Something like mirth tickled him, making his lips quirk. "Should I challenge you to a game, Miss Smith?"

He thought his challenge would go unmet, that she would turn him down and step away, claiming to be much too poor a player to be able to do such a thing, but much to her astonishment, she rose and nodded. "Is this it over here?" she asked, walking closer to the fire where the chess set was already set up and waiting. "Do you mind particularly if I choose the white?"

Quite sure that she was bluffing, John waved a hand. "Of course." He waited for her to laugh, to turn around and state that she was only pretending that she could play and that, of course, she could do no such thing – but she then sat down and eyed her pieces carefully, looking over each one of them.

Slowly, he came towards her, sitting down opposite. Still, she did not turn him away, still, she did not tell him that it was all just a pretense.

"Shall we begin?" she asked, in a slightly firmer voice. "White begins, of course."

If John was astonished at the beginning of his chess match, he was dumbfounded when, one hour later, he was quickly put into check. Staring at the board, he attempted to make one more final move, only for Miss Smith to put him to checkmate.

"I think I win," Miss Smith murmured, her blue eyes alight with laughter as she looked into his face and saw his utter astonishment. "Should you care for another game, your grace?"

He shook his head, hardly able to believe that such a slip of a girl had been able to do what so many of his friends had been unable to do. He could not even recall the last time he had been put in check!

"You have done wonderfully, Miss Smith, and you have surprised me with your skill," he admitted, still unable to lift his eyes from the board. "Well done."

She colored prettily, her eyes dancing. "Thank you, your grace. I look forward to our next game, whenever that may be."

John nodded, unable to rise as she walked away from him, staring at the chessboard in front of him. There was more to Miss Smith than he had first realized and, perhaps, she might bring a little happiness to his life in her own way, if only he would let her.

CHAPTER SEVEN

"Elouise?"

Pushing the bedchamber door open a crack, Laura was surprised to find it empty, with no sign of either Elouise or her maid. Frowning, she made sure to check inside the wardrobe and the dressing room, thinking that perhaps Elouise was intending to hide until Laura managed to find her.

But there was no sign.

"Elouise?" she called again, her voice echoing around the room. "Elouise, where are you?"

Stepping out of the bedroom, she pulled the door tightly shut behind her and began to descend the stairs, wondering if her charge had chosen to eat breakfast in the dining room, which would be, of course, rather unusual for her. However, there was only Lady Alice within, who, with a warm smile, informed her that Elouise had been encouraged to go to the stables that morning.

"Oh?" Laura murmured, coming a little further into

the room. "I did not think she would come downstairs alone to break her fast with you but I am glad to see that she has done so."

Lady Alice smiled, her eyes warm. "It shows, I think, that she is very comfortable here with us."

A warm delight spread across Laura's heart. "Yes," she agreed, softly. "I think it does."

There was silence for a moment, where Laura was caught up with thoughts as to Elouise's return to the orphanage, where the other twelve girls would be waiting to hear all about what her visit to the Duke's home had been like. Would Elouise be glad to go back? She did not think that she would, given that she herself did not much look forward to returning there.

"I believe," Lady Alice said, quietly, interrupting Laura's thoughts, "that my brother is with Elouise."

That startled Laura greatly, turning to look at Lady Alice who was smiling gently, her eyes bright with happiness.

"Truly?" Laura whispered, a little unsure what to make of this. "He asked her to go with him, did he?"

"He did indeed!" Alice declared, sounding more than thrilled. "He came to join me for breakfast and, on finding Elouise here began to discuss with her what she liked the most about being here. When he discovered that she has been eager to visit the horses but has been somewhat fearful in doing so since they are rather large beasts and she does not know what to do about them, he proposed that they go together." She laughed at Laura's astonishment. "I confess I was as surprised as you, but I held my tongue and waved them off, truly delighted for her. I cannot express to you in mere words how relieved I was to see a smile of happiness on my brother's face as he walked out with Elouise. It was truly a sight to behold."

Laura drew in a long breath, feeling a smile spread across her own face in response. "I am very glad to hear it, Lady Alice. I know you have been longing for this day."

"It is only the very beginning, I know, Miss Smith," Lady Alice said, carefully. "And I need to make sure not to push him, but I do believe that this is the beginning of a wonderful moment with Elouise. I am so very glad that you came to be a part of our lives, Miss Smith."

"You are most welcome," Laura replied, not quite sure what else to say. "You have been very generous towards us and I will not forget it."

Lady Alice's eyes twinkled. "Should you wish to go and ensure that Elouise is being well taken care of, then I am quite sure the Duke will not object. He has spoken of nothing else other than his astonishment at how you managed to beat him at chess. Apparently, no-one has managed to do so for many years!"

Laura blushed, her gaze dropping to the floor. "I confess that I have always enjoyed reading and challenging my mind," she said, as Lady Alice nodded approvingly. "I do not have a good deal of time to myself but the time I *do* have, I have always put to good use."

"Well, you have certainly caught my brother's attention," Lady Alice replied, with a chuckle. "I am sure he will be just as glad to see you as Elouise."

Bobbing a quick curtsy, Laura took her leave of Lady Alice and hurried down towards the stables, her mind turning over as she thought of all that Lady Alice had told her. Could it be true? Was this truly the beginning of the Duke's transformation? She had never expected him to do anything of the sort, having been so frustrated with Elouise's presence here only a few days ago, but mayhap something she had said had finally forced him to consider the matter without the presence of anger. Whatever the reason, she was almost deliriously glad that Elouise was with the Duke at this present moment – glad for them both, for it would take away Elouise's fear of the man and, for his sake, show him that life could be a good deal better when there were children about. She knew that herself, for even when things had been hard, when Mary Sanders had been overbearing and almost cruel, she had found happiness in her work of caring for the orphaned girls.

Stepping outside into the cool morning air and wishing that she had thought to bring a shawl with her, Laura quickly made her way towards the stables, stopping dead when she heard the sound of Elouise giggling.

Her heart lifted and, for a moment, she thought to turn around and head back into the house, for fear that she would disturb the Duke and Elouise. But then the longing in her heart grew to a fever pitch and she could not prevent her legs from walking a little further forward, until, finally, she caught sight of them both.

"That's the way," the Duke was saying, deftly cutting another slice from the apple that he held. "Keep your hand flat and hold it steadily. This old boy will not bite you. He is the most gentle natured beast I have ever owned."

Again, came the wonderful sound of Elouise's giggle as the horse snuffled at her palm, carefully taking the apple slice from her. Laura clasped her hands tightly together at her heart, finding the scene almost dream-like. This was truly a wonderful moment.

The Duke chuckled as Elouise asked for another slice, telling her that this was the last one, even though Cartwright, his old horse, would eat the core also. Laura's smile grew all the wider as Elouise presented her palm yet again, before looking up into the Duke's face with shining eyes. Laura felt her heart stop dead in her chest for a moment, seeing the Duke's face completely transformed as he smiled. He became an entirely different man, warm and friendly, instead of the anger and frustration that she had come to expect from him.

It was then that the Duke spotted her, turning his head just a little as he caught her eye. Laura felt a spike of embarrassment shoot through her, as though she ought not to have intruded on them both and turned to leave – only for the Duke to call her name.

"Miss Smith, good morning!"

She had no choice but to turn back to him, seeing the slight redness in his cheeks and realizing that he too was a little embarrassed at having been spotted.

"Your grace," she murmured, inclining her head. "I am sorry for intruding. I did not know where Elouise had gone and thought to come in search of her."

"Oh, Miss Smith!" Elouise breathed, still with that wondrous look in her eyes. "I have been having such a marvelous time. I have fed Cartwright here and the Duke has shown me all of his horses one after the other, although I was too afraid to go near any of them."

The Duke chuckled, and Laura felt her heart lift all

the more.

"I realized that Elouise is truly afraid of the big creatures, which is not surprising when they are so large and she is so little," he said, with a warm smile. "But Cartwright here is very docile, and Elouise has done marvelously well." His eyes caught hers, his mouth in a lop sided smile. "Would you care to be introduced?"

Laura hesitated. "I do not wish to intrude all the more, your grace."

"It would not be an intrusion, I assure you."

Her eyes caught his and were warmed by them, seeing them flare just a little.

"Very well, then," she murmured and moved closer.

The next hour was spent most enjoyably, with Elouise introducing Laura to each of the Duke's horses, although she occasionally had to look to him for help. The Duke was most obliging which brought Laura even more joy, truly finding him to be a remarkably changed man.

"You are staring at me, Miss Smith."

She flushed and looked away as Elouise bounded forward, having found another apple and fully intending to feed it to Cartwright whether or not the Duke approved of it.

"You are wondering if it is the same man who stands before you now," the Duke continued, with just a hint of mirth in his voice. "Yes, I am afraid that it is, Miss Smith. A man who has taken heed of what both you and my sister have said to me and thought to try a slightly different approach with Elouise."

Her eyes sought his and she saw nothing but truth in them. "And?" she asked, softly. "What are the results of your different approach, your grace?"

The Duke hesitated for a moment, before nodding to himself. "I would say, Miss Smith, that the results are very pleasing," he admitted, in a very quiet voice. "In fact, one would go so far as to say that one is rather surprised at the joy such a simple thing as feeding Cartwright an apple or two can bring."

"I think that is to do with the company more than anything else," Laura ventured, still feeling somewhat cautious around him. "She is a very good child, your grace."

There was a few minutes of silence as both Laura and the Duke watched Elouise carefully, both smiling and laughing intermittently as Elouise fed Cartwright the apple and then attempted to stroke him, only for him to go in search of yet more treats. She was laughing and patting his velvet nose, all the while talking to him in a gentle tone.

"I think you have conquered her fear very well, your grace," Laura said softly, looking fondly over at Elouise. "She will be back at Cartwright's side any chance she can get!"

The Duke smiled, but it was not in Elouise's direction. Rather, it was directed towards her and, for the first time, Laura felt her heart suddenly blossom open towards the Duke. It was inexplicable and more than a little foolish, so she tossed it aside, drew in a deep breath and turned her gaze back towards Elouise.

"And you, Miss Smith?"

"What of me, your grace?" she asked, still keeping her gaze fixed on Elouise.

"Do you care much for horses?"

Biting her lip, she shook her head, surprised to see faint disappointment on the Duke's face. "What I mean to say, your grace, is that I have not been near nor even ridden a horse since I was very young. It is not something that is easily available to me."

The Duke nodded slowly, the disappointment fading away. "I quite understand, Miss Smith," he murmured. "I don't suppose that you would consider allowing me to aid you in this matter, just as I have done with Elouise?"

She looked up at him sharply. "I do not fear horses, your grace."

Again, that smile that sent a flood of warmth to her heart.

"No, indeed, Miss Smith. What I meant to say was that I thought of riding out with you, if that would bring you any sort of happiness. I know it has been some time since you last rode, but I am sure it would come back to you very quickly."

For no inexplicable reason, her stomach filled with butterflies.

The Duke shrugged, clearly a little nonplussed at her silence. "It was just a suggestion, Miss Smith. Think on it."

"What must she think on?"

Laura made to tell Elouise, who had come running over to them both, that it was not polite to eavesdrop, only for the Duke to chuckle and pat Elouise's shoulder.

"You must help me in this Elouise," he said, with a

smile. "I am trying to convince Miss Smith to come out riding with me one day soon, but she has stated that she has not ridden in some years!"

Elouise's face lit up. "Oh, but I am sure that you could remember how to do it again, Miss Smith," she exclaimed, tugging a little too hard on Laura's arm. "The Duke has already shown me that I do not need to be afraid of his horses and I am certain that he can show you the very same thing."

It was on the tip of Laura's tongue to explain, in a somewhat frustrated tone that she was not afraid of horses, but at the sound of the Duke's quiet chuckling, she resigned herself to the fact that yes, she was going to have to do as both he and Elouise apparently wanted.

"Very well," she said, with a small sigh. "I shall attempt to come out riding with you one day soon, your grace, but I must beg of you not to expect too much of me."

To her surprise, the Duke appeared to be delighted with this news, for his smile spread from ear to ear, his dark brown eyes suddenly warm and filled with light.

"I shall expect nothing and be as much help as I am able," he promised, as Elouise jumped up and down, clearly delighted with this news. "Shall we say tomorrow?"

Tomorrow felt a little too soon for Laura but she could not exactly refuse, since they had very little else planned.

"I am sure my sister will be more than delighted to spend an hour or two with Elouise, so you need not concern yourself in that regard," the Duke continued, taking her silence for worry over Elouise. "We can go at whatever time of day suits you best, Miss Smith."

"The morning," Laura found herself saying, as they began to walk back towards the estate. "Shall we say around eleven o'clock?"

The Duke beamed. "Wonderful," he said, as a lock of dark brown hair flopped over his forehead. "I look forward to it, Miss Smith."

Laura tried to smile as Elouise began to chatter excitedly, capturing the Duke's attention. She did not feel in the least bit excited, but was rather fearful – not of the riding, for she was sure that as soon as she put her foot in the stirrup, she would remember it all – but about spending time in the Duke's company. Seeing him so altered had, for whatever reason, had a very strange effect on her, where she found her pulse racing inexplicably, her breath catching in her chest when he'd directed his smile towards her. She did not want to feel such ridiculous things for the man who was only to have a brief appearance in her life. She could not allow herself to have any kind of feelings towards him, even if she was glad to see the change in him.

"It has been a wonderful morning, your grace," Elouise said, happily, taking the Duke's arm with one somewhat grubby hand. "Thank you."

Laura felt herself smile as the Duke looked down at her, his expression gentle.

"Thank you, Elouise," the Duke murmured, gently. "I too have had a wonderful morning."

Elouise glowed.

CHAPTER EIGHT

John could not explain the sudden change that had come over him, but he was glad of it. He felt the change in his thoughts the minute he had decided to seek out Miss Smith and ask her forgiveness. He decided then that yes, he would try and improve his attitude to the appearance of both Miss Smith and little Elouise in his home. It was as though his days suddenly grew brighter, as though the sun became more plentiful. In making an effort to step out from the shadows, he had somehow managed to return to the light.

It was an ongoing battle, however, to remain so. The shadows of the past threatened to cling to him all the more as he struggled to continue on as he had been, trying to forge a new path for his life. The presence of Elouise – and even that of Miss Smith had proven to be a blessing to him rather than the burden he had anticipated.

He smiled to himself as he pulled on his riding boots, recalling just how much effort it had taken to encourage

Miss Smith into coming out riding with him. He had not meant to ask her such a thing but all of a sudden, he had found himself blurting out those words with no easy way to take them back. How her eyes had flared as she'd looked up at him, clearly astonished that he, a Duke, would ask a lowly orphanage girl to go riding with him.

A stab of shame thrust its way into his heart. He had spoken harshly to her before, when he had railed at her and Elouise for playing indoors and the regret of what he had said still lingered. He had brought her background and her status in life into question, as though somehow, he considered himself to be better in every way, simply because he was one of the aristocracy. John had to admit that, yes, he still often considered himself to be of higher intellect than his tenants, with better judgment and considerations, but was that because they had simply never had the opportunities he had? It did not behoove him to think so highly of himself, he realized, for Miss Smith had shown him all too well that there were many things that he lacked. Intelligence meant very little compared to a gentle and warm heart. Kindness and generosity were what made a man, not the consideration that one was better than everyone else.

Heat crept into his face as he rose, brushing down his already immaculate coat. Yes, he had already apologized to Miss Smith, but still, the need to prove to her that he no longer thought in such a way pushed at him. Perhaps that was why he had wanted to go out riding with her, to prove that he could be generous towards her as well as to Elouise.

Or perhaps you simply enjoy her company.

CHAPTER 8

The thought had him pausing, mid-stride, before he continued down the hallway towards the front door. Yes, he had to admit that Miss Smith intrigued him, but that was simply because she had beaten him at chess and even now, some days later, the surprise of that moment had not yet worn off. He wanted to find out all he could about her to satisfy his curiosity, that was all. That *had* to be all.

"Ah, Miss Smith!"

John noticed, and subsequently ignored, the way his heart leaped in his chest as he came across Miss Smith waiting for him at the stables. She smiled a little tremulously at him, clearly rather anxious about the whole thing. John smiled back appreciatively, taking her in. She was quite beautiful, he had to admit, with her dark tresses and stunningly blue eyes. Her slender figure was shown off wonderfully in the emerald green habit, although she was currently worrying her lip with her teeth as she stood patiently waiting for him.

"You need not be nervous, Miss Smith," he said quietly, inclining his head as he approached her. "I have the gentlest mare selected for you. She is quiet and docile and will make a marvelous ride, I am sure of it."

Another smile tugged at her lips, but none of the anxiety left her eyes. "Thank you, your grace."

"'Royston' will do, if you please," he replied, growing a little weary of the formality between them.

She blushed. "No, indeed, your grace. I could not."

"I think you must," he stated, with another warm smile. "Truly, Miss Smith, I do not wish for any such formality between us, not when we are quickly becoming good friends."

Her blush darkened her cheeks all the more and John felt his own heart grow warm as she looked up at him, her lips caught in a slightly unsure smile.

"Very well," she murmured. "Then I must hope, Royston, that you recall just how uncertain I am of riding and have not planned a particularly long ride this morning."

He chuckled. "Ah, but I have a little more faith in you than you do yourself, it seems! I thought to show you my estate, Miss Smith. It is wider and longer than what one can see, even from the highest window in the manor house, and has many wonderful features that I am sure you will appreciate. Besides which," he continued, seeing her continuing uncertainty, "we will be able to ride at whatever pace you are comfortable with, and need not fear coming across any other riders or neighbors as we go."

They were at the stables now and Miss Smith, looking a little less concerned, nodded.

"Thank you, your grace – I mean, Royston."

Chuckling, he ushered her inside and, within a few minutes, Miss Smith was getting acquainted with her mount, a beautiful white and grey mare named Molly.

"You see, Miss Smith? You are doing wonderfully well!"

The look of concentration on Miss Smith's face made him laugh, although he tried his very best to keep it hidden from her.

"I can see that you are laughing at me, Royston, and I beg that you would not," Miss Smith muttered, through tight lips. "It is taking me all my strength to remain seated in this strange position."

He chuckled again. "I know that side saddle is not what you are used to, Miss Smith, but it will become just as natural to you in time as sitting astride."

"Astride is what I remember," Miss Smith replied, her mare finally catching up to his stallion. "This is an entirely new situation for me."

Again the urge to laugh seized him but, forcing himself to remain quite nonchalant, he managed to wipe any trace of mirth from his face.

"You are doing very well, Miss Smith," he said, wanting to encourage her. "Now, if you will give me your attention for a moment, you will be able to see the large lake that shimmers in the sunlight. There, to your left."

Her sharp intake of breath told him that she had spotted it and a feeling of appreciation for her began to wrap itself around his heart all over again.

"My goodness," she breathed, her eyes wide as she looked at it. "You have a beautiful estate, I must say. Can we reach the lake easily?"

He looked at her. "Do you wish to go there?"

"I do." Her eyes lifted to his for a moment. "If that is not too much out of your way, of course. I don't mean to command this trip, Royston."

His lips quirked as he looked back at her, seeing her concern and smiling broadly so that it was chased away. "You are doing no such thing, my dear," he murmured, quietly. "Just so long as you are not growing chilled, for I am aware that this morning is not particularly warm, although I am glad that the sun has come out."

"I am not cold in the least," she declared, sounding thrilled that he was to take her to the lake itself. "Thank you, Royston."

"Not at all, Miss Smith," he murmured, before leading the way.

Some time later and John made to help Miss Smith to mount her horse again, only for her to shake her head.

"I can do it myself, I am sure," she said, her eyes turning away from his as a spark of color caught her cheeks. "Really, there is no need."

Something caught him, something sent a thrill of excitement through his veins and, before she could protest any further, he had caught her about the waist. She gasped, his hands tight around her and he lingered there for just a moment too long, looking down into her face and wondering why he felt such a deep, inexplicable longing – although quite what for, he could not say. Then, clearing his throat, he lifted her up into the saddle, keeping his eyes lifted whilst she hastily rearranged her skirts.

"Thank you, Royston," Miss Smith said, rather breathlessly. "Although I did say that I was certain I could do so myself."

He laughed, turning his back on her so that he might mount his own horse. "Indeed, Miss Smith, but that is only when you have ridden astride. To ride side saddle requires an entirely different way of mounting." The blood in his veins was burning hot, the desire to have her in his arms again growing stronger and stronger with every moment that passed. It was quite a ridiculous notion, for they barely knew one another, but even as he tried to give himself a stern talking to, the desire grew all the more.

"Might I ask," Miss Smith said, as he turned his horse's nose back towards the manor house. "Might I ask if you often come here?"

Shaking his head, John chose to keep the truth from her for the moment, not wishing to disclose that he had not come near the lake for almost two years. In fact, he had barely left the manor house since his wife and child had died. "No," he said, slowly, his tone now a little lackluster. "I have not come to the lake particularly often."

Her face clouded. "Oh. I apologize if I ought not to have asked, Royston."

He shrugged, trying to push the sharp stab of pain to one side. "There is nothing for you to apologize for, Miss Smith. The truth is that I have not enjoyed such pleasures since the death of my wife and child. It is only due to your company – and the company of Elouise – that I have finally seen a spark of light. The truth is, Miss Smith, it is exactly as you said. I needed to change how I viewed the girl and, in doing so, I have found the small beginnings of what might lead to true, genuine happiness and contentment, although I will never forget my wife nor the child that was to be mine."

He did not look at her but turned his face away, as though not seeing her would help contain the anger and upset that pierced him.

"I was angry for a long time," he murmured, half to himself. "On occasion, I still am. I question why something so wonderful, something that could have been so beautiful, was taken from me without warning before I even had a chance to greet him – or her. I have not let myself believe that I could have such a thing again, believing that I ought not to replace them both."

"I do not think that, in marrying again and begetting an heir, that you would be doing so." Miss Smith's voice was quiet and thoughtful, her words clearly spoken but with a gentle tenderness that bound the wounds in his heart. "They will live on in your memory, Royston. To have happiness in this life with another, to fill your house with children, will not be to turn your back on the past. It will simply be choosing to step away from your grief. There is nothing wrong with seeking happiness, your grace."

"Then why do I feel as though there is?"

He had not intended to sound so desperate, had not intended to turn to her and ask her such pronounced questions, but having never truly spoken so openly to another living soul, he found that he could not. It was as if he expected Miss Smith to have the answers he required, so that he himself would not have to seek them out himself, going over and over them in his mind.

Miss Smith did not look particularly put out by being asked such a question and instead simply looked back at him with a small, understanding smile on her face.

"I think," she said, carefully. "It is because you have been in a dark place for so long, my lord. You have had the darkness pervade every part of you, winding itself around your heart and mind. It will take time to remove its chains from you, but it is not a quest you should turn from. It is a victory you *can* succeed in, if you would but trust your own strength and know that those alongside you wish to do nothing more than aid you."

"And that includes you," he said, thickly, feeling his heart tighten with a sudden, sharp ache that was something between pain and relief.

Her smile was warm, her expression gentle. "Of course, that includes me, your grace. I will do whatever I can to aid you in this, should you need me."

Clicking to his horse, John said nothing for a few minutes but allowed them to ride in silence, thinking through everything the lady had said. Everything she said spoke of understanding, as though she had been in the place where he stood now.

"You remember your parents, then?"

The question was forceful, springing from the thoughts swirling around his mind.

Miss Smith looked a little surprised but nodded. "Yes, of course. I was young enough to not truly understand what had occurred but old enough to have some good memories of the time I had with them. It is an ongoing grief, Royston, to lose both your parents in one awful moment." Her lips quivered, and she turned her head to look away from him as if she did not want him to see her weakness.

"My father died only a few months after my mother," he said, softly, "although they were both of many years and had lived a very good life. It was as if my father could not contemplate life here on this earth without her, even though their marriage was an arrangement between both families."

There was nothing but the sound of horse's hooves on the stony path for a moment or two as Miss Smith appeared to contemplate what he had said.

"You do not believe that there can be genuine affection in an arrangement, then?" she asked, her cheeks a little pink.

A rueful smile caught his lips. "There was not in my own, Miss Smith."

Her blush deepened. "Oh. I see. I cannot imagine such a state of being, Royston, but then again, that is because such a thing does not occur in Smithfield Market."

A little interested, he lifted one eyebrow. "One can marry whoever one pleases?"

"Of course."

"And...." He stopped, realizing what he was about to ask and consider just how inappropriate it would be to do so. He could not ask her if she had any considerations to marry in the near future, feeling heat rising up his chest as he turned his eyes back to the path and away from Miss Smith.

"Perhaps in the future, when it comes time for you to consider your own path, you might find a lady who will bring you the same happiness your own parents had in their lives," she murmured, quietly. "I do hope that for you, your grace."

"You are very sweet to say so," he replied, quietly. "Thank you, Miss Smith. I shall be sorry to say goodbye to you when it is time for you to return."

The curve of her lips dropped and the light faded

from her eyes. "Indeed, I shall be sorry too, although I must return to the rest of the girls who need me."

His interest grew. "And how many have you at this present moment?"

"Twelve," she said, heavily. "And that does not include Elouise." Shaking her head, her lips caught in a wry smile. "I ought not to complain, but I do worry about them. Mary Sanders is often inclined to do nothing more than consider the practical workings of the orphanage and without my presence to temper that, I fear that she may have gone a little overboard. There is another in my place, Helen, but she is only new and may not quite understand how best to deal with Mary Sanders."

John watched her closely, seeing her concerned expression and felt his affection and regard for the lady grow. "You truly do care for these girls, do you not, Miss Smith?"

She looked at him sharply. "Of course I do. How could I not? I have been in their situation. I know the pain and the grief and the terror that comes with being in such a dark place. I have a responsibility towards them even though it is, I confess, very difficult at times."

"Difficult?"

Sighing, Miss Smith looked away. "I ought not to complain, Royston, for I have employment and food and a roof over my head and that is more than many can say. But yes, the work is hard, and the hours are long and I often find myself bone weary. To have come here and experienced what life is like for those who have plenty has been a respite for me and I am truly grateful for it."

"Then perhaps you will have to come back at the

same time next year," he said, with a small murmur of satisfaction in his heart at the idea. "So that you do not fade away to nothing."

She laughed then, the tension gone from her and he found himself joining in. Their conversation turned to brighter things and they made a very merry pair as they returned to the stables at Royston manor.

CHAPTER NINE

As the weeks passed, Laura discovered that the change in the Duke of Royston had, despite her doubts, become permanent. He was laughing and smiling a good deal more now, his eyes bright and warm whenever they lingered on either herself or Elouise. It was truly a wonderful transformation and Laura knew that everyone in the house – staff included – were glad to see it.

"Miss Smith?"

She looked up from her book to see none other than the Duke and Elouise hurrying towards her, Elouise's face beaming with the widest of smiles. She rose from where she had been idly swinging on the garden swing, her coat warming her as the midday sun tried its best to shine with more strength. Her heart quickened as the Duke's eyes caught her own, his smile growing softer as she held his gaze. Truly, he was a handsome gentleman and even though she berated herself for letting her foolish heart flutter in such a ridiculous fashion, she knew that to even attempt to prevent herself from feeling such things would fail completely.

"My dear Miss Smith!" the Duke called, as they approached her. "We have made an excellent discovery this afternoon."

"Oh?"

Elouise bounded up to her, throwing her arms around Laura's waist and making her stagger back as she attempted to keep her footing. A strong hand caught her arm, helping her to stand upright and, as she looked up to thank the Duke, found his hand gentling on her arm, remaining there for just a fraction too long.

"Thank you, Royston," she murmured, quietly. "It appears Elouise has something of considerable importance to tell me!"

The Duke chuckled and let go of her completely. "That she does," he agreed, putting one hand on Elouise's shoulder. "Do you want to tell Miss Smith what we found today?"

"We were exploring," Elouise said, delightedly, looking up at Laura with wide, excited eyes. "Royston has been helping me to ride the little mare Bluebell, and we wandered into the woods for a time and came across an old, enchanted ruin!"

Laura's lips twitched as she caught the Duke's eye, realizing both that he had allowed the child to call him 'Royston' and that he had also encouraged her in her wild imagination.

"An enchanted ruin, you say?" she asked, bending down to look into Elouise's face. "How wonderful! What was so enchanted about it?"

Elouise launched into a wild and wonderful description of the ruin, believing there to be all sorts of creatures nearby and stating that, were they to see it in the darkness, in the middle of the night, then most likely they would discover some enchanted creatures, such as had never been seen before. Laura listened attentively, although she glanced from time to time up at the Duke, seeing the way he was smiling gently at them both and feeling herself grow all the fonder of him. He had chosen to linger on in the light, to find a way forward for himself that would require strength, courage, and fortitude. At times, she saw him slip back into the world he had only just come from, his eyes growing dim, the smile fading from his face. She would do her best to catch his eye, to engage him in conversation, to smile at him and then, with an effort, he would pull himself back to the present. She knew that the sadness and the grief would always be a part of him, but it did not have to overwhelm him any longer. The strength and courage he possessed made her respect him all the more.

"My goodness, Elouise," she exclaimed, as her charge came to the end of her story about the ruin. "You have had a marvelous afternoon, haven't you? I trust that you have thanked the Duke for his company today?"

Elouise did not simply smile, look up at the Duke and thank him graciously, but rather she threw her arms around his waist and hugged him tightly, her face scrunched up in an expression of sheer delight.

"Thank you ever so much, Royston," she exclaimed, as the Duke's lips curved into a surprised, but pleasant, smile. "I have had the best of days. I am already looking forward to our ride again tomorrow. Do you think we could go back there? And do you think that Miss Smith could join us?"

Her arms loosened around his waist and she looked up at him inquisitively, hope burning in her expression.

"If Miss Smith is willing, then I would be delighted for her to join us," the Duke replied, warmly, throwing Laura a glance that sent sparks flying into her very soul. "I think another opportunity for Miss Smith to ride would be a very pleasant one."

She laughed, shaking her head. They had gone out riding a good many times over the last few weeks and she had enjoyed every bit of it – except the side saddle. "No matter how much you try to induce a love of the side saddle in me, Royston, I do not think it shall ever come to fruition. I am much too uncouth, I'm afraid."

He snorted. "Nonsense. You do very well, Miss Smith. Tomorrow it is."

"Tomorrow," she agreed, as Elouise let out a whoop of delight. "Now, shall we go in for some refreshments, Elouise? I am sure you must be hungry."

"I am," Elouise agreed and, without hesitating, ran full pelt back towards the manor house, leaving Laura and the Duke behind.

Laura let out a small, rueful sigh. "It appears that my teaching on manners is sorely lacking, your grace. I do apologize."

He chuckled and offered her his arm. "Not in the least, Miss Smith. I find Elouise quite charming just as she is. And, besides which, we are only children once. Shall we walk back together?"

She looked up at him, not quite sure what she was meant to do having never walked with a gentleman before.

"Here," he said, with a small smile that did not hold even the slightest hint of mockery. "Place your hand under my arm and hold on here."

Laura could feel the heat radiate from her face as she did so, realizing that this was something of an intimate connection. She kept her face turned towards the house as they began to walk, not able to look at him as they did so.

"Your sister prepares to leave for London at the beginning of next month," she said, a little hoarsely as her emotions flew all through her, leaving her feeling entirely off balance. "Will you be sorry to see her go?"

There was a short pause. "I do not enjoy the idea of living here alone, no. For when she departs at the end of next month, you and Elouise will return with her, will you not?"

The thought pierced her. "I suppose we will."

His lips thinned, the light disappearing from his eyes.

"Unless, of course," she said, slowly, "there is a reason for the situation, such as it is, to change."

She did not really know what she meant, nor what she was trying to say, but the words kept coming from her regardless.

"I know that Elouise has been very happy here," she continued, her tongue running away with her. "The thought of returning to London is not a happy one for her, your grace." Slipping back into formality, she closed her eyes for a moment, only to let them fly open as she drew in a sharp breath, forcing herself to get a hold of her driving emotions.

"What I mean to say is, Royston, let us not think of such things until they are inevitable," she finished, lamely. "Although I will say that, for myself, I will miss this wonderful place and the delightful company that has come with it."

There then came a few moments of silence as they continued to walk together, their steps slow and careful. Feeling as though she had said far too much and had not been able to express herself coherently, Laura lapsed into silence, frustrated with herself. She had been trying to suggest, in as gentle a way as possible, that the Duke consider adopting Elouise, but in her struggle to speak carefully, had managed to make a complete cake of herself. It was, however, something that she had begun to hope would occur for Elouise, aware of just how close the young girl was becoming to the Duke. It would be terribly painful for her to be ripped away from Royston manor and the Duke himself only to return to London and the orphanage, but if the Duke did not consider adoption to be something he could manage, then there was nothing else for it. Whilst she had tried her best to remind Elouise about their inevitable return to London, Elouise had always shrugged it off, telling Laura that she was much too busy enjoying herself at this present moment to worry about the future.

"I will miss you all terribly," the Duke said slowly, breaking the silence. Laura looked up at him to see his brows furrowing, as though he had been lost in the joy of rediscovered happiness to recall that soon, it would all be coming to a close. "I must consider these matters with a good deal more care."

Her heart lifted with a sudden hope, her lips curving into a glad smile. "Thank you, Royston. I know you will." Glancing up, she saw Lady Alice at one of the windows and raised a hand in greeting. Lady Alice waved back, a small smile on her face.

"Your sister intends to find herself a husband this Season, I hear," Laura continued, changing the subject entirely. "She has three suitors, she told me, and you think all of them will suit her which means she has the choice entirely left to her."

The Duke chuckled, his eyes lighting with mirth. "Indeed, is that what she said?" He shook his head, still laughing. "My dear sister is right to say that she has three suitors but as to my own thoughts on the matter, I find them quite changed, I'm afraid."

"Oh?" Laura glanced up at him, feeling her own lips spread into a smile at his apparent humor.

"Well," he continued, as they entered the house. "I have you to thank for that, Miss Smith. When Alice first came to me with news of her suitors, I did not think much of it. I considered that she was wise enough to choose her own husband, caring nothing for her future. Whilst I still believe that she *is* wise enough to do that, I intend to now take a much more interest in these three particular gentlemen. I must look into their backgrounds, their families, and their financial situation before I am certain they are worthy of her."

That brought Laura a good deal of satisfaction. "I do believe that is all that Lady Alice is hoping for, Royston," she said, softly, as they came to a halt in front of the butler and maid, who took their gloves, hats, and coats. "I think she does wish for your involvement."

"Then she shall get it!" the Duke exclaimed, as the butler and maid stepped away. "Although I am not so certain she will be as pleased with my involvement when she sees just how scrutinizing I will be!"

"Oh no!" Laura laughed, as they made their way along the corridor together. "I shall be to blame for this now also, shall I not?"

The Duke chuckled, stopped and turned to take her hand in his. Without their gloves, his fingers were warm and soft, yet held a strength that seemed to reverberate up her arm. Heat crept up her spine, her face flushing a gentle pink as he bowed over it.

"I must go to my study and attend to some business, Miss Smith," he murmured, his humor now replaced with something a good deal more intense. "Thank you for walking with me. I have, as always, enjoyed conversing with you, Miss Smith."

"And I you," she breathed, her whole body suddenly bursting with life as his lips gently pressed to the back of her hand. And then, as he raised his head and let go of her hand, she felt her limbs suddenly weak, as though overcome by what had occurred and by what she had felt.

"Until dinner, Miss Smith."

She managed to smile and nod, wondering if she would need to lean on the wall in order to remain standing. "Until dinner, Royston."

He stepped away from her, walking the short distance until he reached his study. Laura forced her weak legs to walk forward, putting on the appearance of calmness until, finally, when the study door shut, she was able to press one hand against the wall for support as she dragged in a long breath.

"Goodness," she breathed, her body now tingling all over. "This is getting quite out of hand!"

Closing her eyes, she dragged in a few calming breaths, forcing her heart to quieten itself as she paused there. Her reaction to the feel of his lips against her hand had been extreme, sending a wave of desire crashing all through her. She'd let her mind jump to the idea of having herself wrapped in his arms, of lifting her face to his – and then, of course, recalled that she was nothing more than a poor orphaned young lady and he a Duke of the realm.

The library door opened, and Laura forced herself to stand upright, making slow steps towards the door just as Lady Alice poked her head out.

"Ah, there you are, Miss Smith," she said, smiling. "I was wondering if you would join me. Might you care for some tea?"

"I was just going to see about Elouise," Laura replied, hoping her voice did not betray her. "Although I have very little idea where she has gone to!"

Lady Alice chuckled and beckoned Laura inside. "The maid found her, and she was marched up to her room with the promise that she would have all sorts of delicious goodies once she had allowed herself to be bathed properly. The maid declared, in as loud a voice as she could, that the child smelled of horses and mud! I'm afraid I had to agree."

Laura chuckled and walked into the library, ringing the bell for tea. "I'm afraid Elouise is still not quite used to regularly bathing but I am sure she will become used to it."

Lady Alice laughed softly. "I think she will have to, if she is to remain here."

That had Laura turning quickly, sending Lady Alice a sharp glance. Her hopes flared all over again. "I was just speaking to Royston – I mean, the Duke – about such matters," she said, quickly, sitting down opposite Lady Alice and keeping her gaze steady. "Do you think there is a chance that the Duke might consider keeping her on here?"

Lady Alice smiled softly. "Are you asking me if I believe my brother is considering adopting the girl, Miss Smith?"

Not quite sure that she was not overstepping the bounds of propriety, Laura gave Lady Alice a slightly jerky nod. "Yes, I believe I am," she said, hoarsely. "Forgive me if I ought not to be asking such things but –"

"There is nothing to apologize for, Miss Smith," Lady Alice said, warmly. "I have every intention of encouraging my brother to adopt the girl, for I believe he is beginning to be truly happy once more. The presence of Elouise here has brought such a big change about him that I cannot see how he could send her away now."

Laura nodded slowly, her fingers knotting together in her lap as she considered it. "I am very glad," she said, slowly, "for I know that Elouise does also care for the Duke in her own way. I have not seen the girl so happy ever since she first came to the orphanage."

CHAPTER 9

Lady Alice beamed. "I am glad to hear you say that. It appears that they have both been very good for each other – although, I will say, Miss Smith, that you have had an equally important role in the improvement of his temperament."

A slight flush caught Laura's cheeks. "I do not think that –"

"Did you know," Lady Alice interrupted, halting Laura's excuses. "That he has never once come out riding with either me or a friend ever since his wife died? In fact, the staff told me that he barely rode at all and, if he did, it was only out of necessity." She tilted her head just a little, regarding Laura carefully. "And now I hear that he has gone out with Elouise, but also with you."

Her flush deepened. "We have ridden out together on occasion," she admitted, carefully. "But I did not realize it was significant."

Lady Alice's smile was gentle. "My dear Miss Smith, I do not want you to mistake the fact that my brother's consideration of you is due to his growing affection. I am quite sure of it, my dear, so you need not look as shocked as all that."

Laura's breath had been taken from her lungs in astonishment, one hand pressed to her heart and the other to her mouth as she looked back steadily at Lady Alice, who was doing nothing more than sitting there quietly, a smile lingering around her mouth.

"No," she whispered, unable to put any strength into her voice. "No, Lady Alice, you are quite mistaken."

Lady Alice laughed softly and shook her head. "No, my dear. I know my brother all too well to think that such consideration of you comes from a place of friendship only. Have you not noticed the way he looks at you? I certainly have. There is a warmth there that is only there for you. The smile on his lips is a tender one. My dear Miss Smith, you must believe me when I tell you that there is a good depth of feeling in my brother's heart for you."

Laura wanted to shake her head, wanted to say that Lady Alice was quite wrong and that nothing of the sort could be the case, but instead she just stared at her blankly.

"Do you think you would consider staying on for a longer time when I return to London?" Lady Alice asked, gently. "It may take my brother a little longer to work out what exactly it is that he thinks and feels and, therefore, what he wishes to occur when it comes to both yourself and Elouise, but I am sure that your future will be here, Miss Smith."

She could not take it in, her breathing coming quick and fast as she looked back at Lady Alice.

"I cannot," she said hoarsely, thinking of the other girls back at the orphanage. "I am nothing more than a poor orphaned lady and he is –"

"You will find that my brother is not typical of the aristocracy, Miss Smith," Lady Alice said, with another smile. "He is fond of children, for one, which is quite the opposite of most gentlemen in the nobility, I'm afraid! He does what he pleases and will not allow the difference in your status to be any kind of burden. You see, Miss Smith, in being a Duke, one is able to care very little for the opinions of others. One does not care what they say or think or do, or even if scandal becomes attached to oneself, simply because of the high title one carries. I am a Duke's sister and therefore must be a *trifle* more careful than my brother, but he does not need to have any considerations of the sort. Mark my words, Miss Smith, you need not fear that he will turn away from you simply because of the distance between you both in terms of status. Can you not see that in how he treats you?"

Laura made to answer, only for there to come a knock at the door and the maid to enter with a tea tray, swiftly followed by a spotless Elouise, who had been washed, dried and dressed and had now come to join them for tea. She was forced to keep her questions to herself, to let her mind spin with all that she had heard from Lady Alice. She could not remain here, could she? Not when the girls at the orphanage needed her. She could not simply abandon them to Mary Sanders, who would not care about anything other than the smooth running of the orphanage whilst neglecting the girls entirely.

Despite that, however, Laura felt her heart burn with a deep, unsettling fire. The truth was that she *did* care for the Duke and had done so for some weeks now. The affection that she felt for him, whilst she had strongly tried to deny it, had been growing steadily and now to hear that he might consider her in the same way she considered him was almost too wonderful to accept. Her heart was torn, knowing that she wanted to stay here with the Duke and Elouise, whilst also longing to return to the orphanage and care for the girls there. They needed her. But did the Duke not need her as well?

Her head began to ache and, quietly, Laura excused

herself, saying that she needed to change for dinner. Lady Alice gave her a small, understanding smile whilst Elouise bounded to her feet to go in search of the book Lady Alice had been reading to her. Quickly, Laura made her way back to her room, suddenly longing to lie down on her bed and rest her head, heavy with thoughts and filled with confusion. What was her future to be? And could she really bring herself to refuse should the Duke ask her to stay on?

Closing her eyes, Laura tried to calm her fractious thoughts, aware that her heart, despite her confusion, was filling with a deep, unrelenting joy at the thought of being in the Duke's arms. Was there even the smallest chance that he might love her? And was that what she felt for him? Having never experienced such an emotion, Laura could not tell what love was supposed to feel like – but if it was to be a deep affection, a genuine respect and an urge to always be in his company, then she could not deny that she felt each of those things with an ever-increasing intensity.

"Good gracious," she murmured aloud, wandering to the window of her bedchamber and looking out at the beautiful grounds beneath. "I think I must love him after all."

CHAPTER TEN

"John?"

Looking up, John saw Alice standing framed in the doorway, her expression a little wary.

"Yes?"

She hesitated. "Might I come in for a moment?"

Nodding, John got to his feet, a little confused as to why his sister appeared so reluctant. "Of course, Alice. You know you are always welcome in here."

She smiled at him, although it did not quite reach her eyes. "Yes. Thank you, John."

"Please." He gestured to the chair by the fire and, after ringing the bell for tea, poured himself a brandy and came to sit down opposite her. Alice still looked rather anxious, the lines on her face a little more pronounced in the firelight. He wanted to rub them away, to relieve her of whatever was upsetting her.

"Did you have an enjoyable day?" she asked, surprising him. "I know you took Elouise to the ruin, for she told me all about it – including the enchantments that were all about!"

He chuckled, the tension broken in a moment. "Yes, indeed. She had a marvelous time – as did I. We are planning to take Miss Smith there tomorrow."

Alice nodded slowly, a look of understanding in her eyes. "John," she began, carefully. "I do not want you to think that I am prying or that I am, in any way, trying to push you in one direction or another, but I must ask –"

She was interrupted by the arrival of the tea tray, which frustrated John a little, given that she had been about to speak to him about whatever was on her mind. It was a good few minutes before she was ready again, her cup of tea gently steaming as she placed it delicately back in the saucer.

"What I wish to ask you, John, is what your intentions are for the girl," Alice said, a little more firmly. "You care for her, that much is obvious, but she will return to the orphanage unless something changes."

His gut twisted, recalling how Miss Smith had said almost the same thing to him. "Have you been talking to Miss Smith about this?"

Alice looked startled. "No," she said, firmly. "I have not asked her opinion on the matter, although I have merely stated that you will have to consider Elouise's future with a good deal of care. I want to ensure that you are doing that, John."

He swallowed hard but shook his head. "The truth is, Alice, I have not been considering it at all." It was as if, with those words, a heavy burden settled itself on his shoulders. "I have not thought of it at all, for I had not realized that their time here with us was coming to an end so soon."

Alice's expression was sympathetic. "She has been a wonderful young lady to have here, John. I know that she has helped bring you out of your misery."

Another sigh escaped him. "Yes, she has," he admitted, pushing his fingers through his hair. "As has Miss Smith."

There came a short silence as Alice looked at him steadily, allowing him some time with his thoughts. He knew what she was suggesting, knew what she was trying to get him to realize and yet still he could not bring himself to say those words aloud.

"Goodness, Alice," he muttered, leaning forward so that his elbows were on his knees, burying his face in his hands. "Why has this only come upon me today?"

A quiet laugh came from her. "Because, my dear brother, you have been caught up in all the happiness that has come with spending time with both Elouise and Miss Smith. You will now have to consider your future with *both* of them."

His head shot up, his breath hitching.

"Yes, John," Alice said, fondly, as though gently rebuking him. "Of course, I know how you feel about Miss Smith, even if you will not say so to me. It is quite obvious that you care for her very dearly, even if you think that you have kept such feelings very well hidden." She chuckled as he stared at her, sitting back in her chair and sipping her tea. "So, tell me, John," she finished, her tension and anxiety now gone completely. "What is it that you are considering? Will you have Elouise with you here for good?"

John let out a long, careful breath. "The truth is, Alice, I am not certain what I ought to do. I do not want Elouise to go, for she is truly a wonderful child, but I cannot abide the thought of Miss Smith returning to London either. But I must question my feelings. Are they strong enough to consider a future with her?"

Alice tipped her head. "Have you felt anything like this before, John? For any of the young ladies you met?"

"No," he said slowly. "But I have not allowed myself to ever become caught up with another, since I always knew I was to marry father's chosen bride for me." Hesitating, he knew he had to admit this out loud. "I will not pretend that I find any of the ladies of my acquaintance to be anything like Miss Smith. She stands entirely on her own two feet, outshining the rest. She may not have all the airs and graces that a genteel young lady is expected to have, but she does not need them for her generous spirit and kind heart means more than any of those supposed qualities."

"It sounds as though you admire her, John."

"I do," he admitted, quietly. "I have a good deal of respect for her. She has not shied away from speaking to me in ways that I needed to hear, even though I did not appreciate that at the time. She has shown me kindness, has shown me more forgiveness than I ever deserved. In short, Alice, she is unlike anyone I have ever known before."

Alice smiled gently. "And she is good for you, John. It is not only Elouise's presence that has brought you back to the man you once were, it is Miss Smith's presence also. I have seen how you have sought her out and I have seen how she looks for you. Trust me when I say there is something in her own heart for you also."

There came a sudden ache in his throat, as though this meant that everything he hoped for, everything he had wanted, was being handed to him. He did not know what to say, breathing hard as he let his gaze fix to the floor, overwhelmed by it all. Until this very moment, he had not realized that he cared so deeply for Miss Smith and yet, here he was, realizing that to have her in his home, to have her by his side, was all he wanted. To have Miss Smith and Elouise would bring his life more happiness than he had ever thought possible.

"I suppose I shall have to consider things long and hard," he muttered quietly, as Alice let out a murmur of agreement. "Thank you for coming to talk to me about this, Alice. I hope you were not concerned that I would refuse to speak to you about these matters!"

His eyes lifted to hers and again he saw the deep concern written in her expression.

"I was concerned," Alice admitted. "I have been prodding you and questioning you for so long, all in the hope of aiding you somehow and, thus far, I have failed. I was unsure as to whether or not you would welcome my intrusion."

Reaching forward, he placed his hand on hers, feeling more appreciation than he could express. "You can never know just how much good you have done me, my dear sister," he said, gently. "You brought Elouise and Miss Smith into my home and look just how much my world has changed. That is all because of you, Alice. I can never thank you enough."

Alice's words continued to linger in John's mind even the next day, when Elouise and Miss Smith rode with him to the ruin in the center of the woods that were a part of his estate. He could not help but feel a sense of contentment as he let Elouise lead the way, with Miss Smith staying close beside her. This was truly what happiness was like, he told himself, realizing that he had not been in danger of slipping back into the darkness for a good few days now. In fact, he had not felt the grief he had been so used to feeling pierce his heart for a long time. The pain and suffering he had been so used to was no longer a part of his daily life and, with that realization came a huge swell of relief.

"And I have you to thank, my dear ladies," he muttered to himself, his eyes lingering on Miss Smith.

"Here we are!" Elouise exclaimed, as the path rounded to the left to reveal what must once have been a fairly large structure of sorts. It had been here ever since John could remember, although no-one really knew what it was. His father had joked once that it had been a place for smugglers and thieves, which had made for many entertaining stories. His mother, of course, had believed that it was an old chapel, where priests had spent time with God so as not to be disturbed by any other living soul and surrounded only by nature. John did not know for certain what it could have been but was glad that Elouise found it as delightful as he had once done.

"Careful now," he chuckled, bringing his stallion to a stop and jumping down before looping the reins loosely over a branch. "Remember, Elouise, a lady always waits for assistance before she attempts to dismount."

Elouise, who had been on the verge of jumping down herself, looked suitably chagrined, even though a mischievous smile escaped her as he took her in his arms to lift her down. Her brown eyes, so like his own, were filled with delight and John could not help but laugh as he put her down, seeing her scurry away into the ruin.

"Do be careful, Elouise!" Miss Smith called, sounding a little anxious. "Royston, there is not anything that could fall on her or the like, is there?"

Smiling at her concern, he shook his head and walked over to her. "No, she is a fairly careful child and I myself spent a good many years climbing all over this when I was but a child myself. You need not worry, Miss Smith."

He held his arms out to her, feeling his heart quickening in his chest as he did so. The thought of having her in his arms sent a fiery warmth all through him, making his breathing catch.

Carefully, she moved forward from her seat and leaned out, her hands on his shoulders. He placed his hands around her waist carefully, helping her to the ground.

Then, time seemed to come to a standstill.

She was still in his arms. He ought to have moved back by now, ought to have let her go but found that he could not. She was so close to him, her hands still resting gently on his shoulders and her mouth a little open as she looked up at him questioningly. All other coherent thought left his mind as he looked into her eyes, seeing the flecks of green spiraling through the blue. Her long dark lashes and dusky pink cheeks only added to her beauty, making him more inclined than ever to keep a hold of her.

"Royston," she breathed, her voice low and husky. "I –"

The urge to kiss her came to him strong and fierce and, before he knew what he was doing, he had lowered his head and pressed his mouth to hers.

Miss Smith responded to him immediately, her hands tightening on his shoulders before moving to wrap around his neck. Angling his head just a little, he pulled her tighter against him, almost entirely overcome with passion. She was warm and sweet, her lips were gentle and soft, making his heart burst with love.

"Miss Smith? You must come and see!"

The sound of Elouise's voice broke them apart. John looked down at Miss Smith with gentle eyes, resting his forehead against hers for just a moment before stepping back. He reluctantly let her go, wishing that they had not been interrupted. There was more that he had wanted to say to her, wanted to explain that this kiss, whilst unexpected, was not something he did without thought.

But it appeared that Miss Smith did not have any kind of anger or frustration at him doing such a thing. Instead, she had a shy smile on her face, her eyes darting up to his face and then back to the ground again. Her cheeks were a rosy red but there was a happiness in her expression that told him his advances were welcomed.

His sister had been right. Miss Smith *did* have a dear affection for him also.

"We will need to talk later, Miss Smith," he murmured, catching her hand for a moment and pressing it lightly. "Perhaps this evening, when we cannot be interrupted?"

She ducked her head for a moment, although he could still see her smile lingering. "Thank you, Royston," she replied, quietly. "I would like that very much."

CHAPTER ELEVEN

*T*heir kiss had been surprising, but Laura did not, for one moment, regret it. The tenderness, the affection that had been shown to her in that one heady moment had spoken to her heart and made it all the more difficult for her to deny that what she felt for the Duke was, in fact, love.

Lady Alice, she was sure, must have known that something had occurred, given the knowing smiles that were sent in both her and the Duke's direction over dinner. It was now late evening and, with Elouise safely off to bed, Laura was walking up and down the library, knowing that she had not yet managed to speak to the Duke in private, as they had hoped. He had been called to his study on some urgent business by his steward and had shot her an apologetic look, which she had accepted graciously.

Her stomach knotted as she tried to find a way to calm her mind, her anxiety riding higher and higher the more she thought of what had occurred between herself and the Duke. Yes, she cared for him – loved him, even – and what he felt for her was no longer undeniable, but could there truly be anything more for them than that? What about her orphanage? What of the other girls that were there, waiting for to return? She could not be selfish and only consider her own future, for that would not be fair or right to them – but yet she was desperate to be a part of the Duke's life. And Elouise.....she had grown so close to Elouise. She felt as though they were almost related in some way or another, and to return to the orphanage without her would be a great wrench. She was quite certain that the Duke would not let Elouise return there, not when they had become so dear to one another. Most likely, he was making certain that all of the arrangements were in place so that he might ask Elouise if she would like to stay in Royston manor for good. Her heart squeezed with both happiness and pain in knowing that, whatever was to happen to Elouise, she would, most likely, have to say goodbye to her. She could not simply forget the other girls.

"Oh, Miss Smith!"

The door opened, and she turned to see the Duke step inside, looking both awkward and relieved to see her.

"Your grace – I mean, Royston," she stammered, a little taken aback to see him clad in only his shirt sleeves and breeches, with neither cravat nor waistcoat. "I do apologize if you intended to come in here for some peace. I can retire, of course."

He smiled at her and closed the door tightly behind him, leaning against it for a moment. "No, my dear Miss

Smith, you shall not go. I know this is very late, but we must consider what...occurred earlier today."

She blushed furiously as he remained where he was, a lopsided smile on his face and a bright look in his eye. He was more relaxed than she had ever seen him, to the point that she became more flustered than ever before. She did not know what to say or what to do so chose to sit down by the fire, putting her hands neatly into her lap. Her gaze remained fixed on him, however, aware of just how quickly her heart beat when he was near, aware of just how much she longed to be in his arms again. These thoughts brought another flush of color to her face, which the Duke saw given the fact that his smile broadened.

"Royston," she began, when the silence stretched out between them. "I am not sure what it is I should say. I confess this is a highly unusual situation and one where I am completely uncertain as to what is expected of me."

Slowly, he pushed himself away from the door and meandered towards her almost lazily, his smile spreading across his face. "I know, Miss Smith. I will be truthful with you and tell you that I too feel the same. Thanks to my dear sister, however, I have been forced to consider my heart and my feelings towards both you and towards Elouise – although they are very different emotions, you understand."

Her cheeks were not going to lose their rosy sheen any time soon, she realized, as heat washed over her again. "I quite understand, Royston. Might I ask what it is you are intending for Elouise?"

"Ah, Miss Smith," he murmured, tenderly, finally coming to sit by her. "You are always so good at considering others before yourself, are you not?" Tugging his chair a little closer, the rug rucking up underneath the legs, he took her hand in his and held it tightly. "You are the most generous-hearted young lady I have ever met, Miss Smith."

"You are very kind to say so," Laura managed to say, her throat growing tight as he leaned ever closer. "But these girls are my life. They are all I have that is precious. In a way, they have become my family and it is my duty, nay, my desire to ensure that their lives are as happy and as content as possible, given the enormous loss that they have each suffered."

The Duke reached up and brushed a finger down her cheek, his eyes fixed on her own. She could almost see into his very soul when she looked into his eyes, aware that there was an intensity within them than she had ever seen before.

"I want you to stay here."

She closed her eyes, feeling as though she was being torn apart.

"I need you, Miss Smith."

Her very bones ached with longing.

"I want to stay, Royston," she admitted, softly, "but I cannot only consider my own wants. It would be unfair to the girls that need me."

He shook his head, still sitting very close to her. "To consider what your heart wants is not selfish, Miss Smith....Laura."

The way he said her name sent shivers up her spine. There was such passion in it, such tenderness that she could hardly bring herself to refuse him.

"I cannot stay, Royston." There was no strength to her voice, hearing it hoarse and cracked as it came from her. Her eyes lowered to the floor, hearing her heart cry out in pain but knowing, nevertheless, that she was doing the right thing.

There was no response from him for a moment and then he rose, in one swift movement, and tugged her to him. Before she could say another word, before she could even take a breath, he had caught her lips in a kiss and, within a moment or two, she was lost.

His hands were tight around her waist and she found herself pressed up against him, her arms around his neck, her fingers twining through his hair of their own volition. This was not a moment she was ever likely to forget, trying her best to show him, through her embrace, just how much she loved him.

"Miss Smith?"

She stumbled back, hearing Elouise's voice. The Duke stepped away at once, keeping his back to the child as she entered the room.

"Elouise," Laura managed to say, her voice sounding rather higher than normal. "Elouise, what are you doing here? You should be in bed."

Elouise rubbed her eyes, looking completely exhausted. "I was scared," she said, simply. "I wanted to find you but you weren't in your bedchamber. I had a bad dream."

Laura, feeling her heart pounding madly in her chest, tried to put on an expression of sympathy but, all the while, felt almost exasperated at the child for appearing out of nowhere and interrupting them both. "Well, come along then. Let me take you back to bed."

She made to step forward to take the child's hand but, to her surprise, Elouise took a few steps further into the library, her eyes settling on the Duke who was, by now, looking at them both with dark eyes.

"What were you doing?"

The child's question brought a heat to her face.

"Elouise," she said firmly. "You ought not to pry into other people's affairs. Come now, this is not something you need to talk about any further."

She tried to take Elouise's hand again but the girl stepped deftly out of reach, planting her hands on her hips. She made an almost comical figure, dressed in her nightgown with her braided hair flipped over one shoulder, her tired eyes a little defiant.

"Miss Smith, I saw you and the Duke. That only happens with....." She trailed off, looking a little embarrassed, although her jaw clenched angrily. "With my mother and father. That's what they used to do and they were married. Is that what you're planning, Miss Smith? Are you going to stay here with the Duke?"

A flush of embarrassment rose in Laura's face and she kept her eyes fixed on the child, unwilling to look back at the Duke for fear of what she would see in his face.

"Elouise," she said firmly, with a good deal more strength. "Your questions are entirely inappropriate. None of this involves you, do you understand?"

She realized at once that she has said this rather badly, seeing Elouise's lip quiver and her eyes fill with tears.

"You need not think, my dear girl, that you are quite unimportant to me. In fact, quite the opposite! However, I will admit that I care for Miss Smith also"

From the look on Elouise's face, Laura realized that the girl had very little understanding of what the Duke meant. She could see that Elouise was confused and even a little scared and, despite her own embarrassment at being caught in such an inappropriate embrace with the Duke, wanted to comfort Elouise as best she could.

Finally managing to catch her hand, she smiled and stepped forward, closer to the girl before bending her knees so that she might look into her face.

"What the Duke means is that he cares for you very much, Elouise, as do I. There is nothing to worry about, nothing to be afraid of. We *both* care about you a great deal. Everything is going to be wonderful, I promise."

Elouise looked back at her for a few moments, before wrenching her hand out of Laura's.

"The only person you care about is yourself, Miss Smith!" she exclaimed, stepping backwards towards the door. "You say you care about me but all the time, you've just been wanting to stay here with the Duke yourself. What about me? Am I going to be sent back to the orphanage while you stay here?"

"That is quite enough, Elouise."

The Duke's voice was loud and firm, his voice bouncing off the walls and echoing around the room. Elouise stopped dead, her eyes wide as she turned her face towards the Duke, tears shimmering in her eyes.

"You are not to speak to Miss Smith in that way," the

Duke said, sternly. "She is only trying to help you and you ought to show her more respect."

A sob ripped through Elouise's chest, tearing at Laura's soul. She stayed exactly where she was, feeling her heart pounding in her chest. She wanted to go to Elouise but didn't know what to say, aware that the Duke's voice had only made things worse than before. It was clear that Elouise was confused by what she had witnessed and had let that confusion turn into anger and upset, to the point that she refused to believe that Laura had her best interests at heart.

"You only care about yourselves!" Elouise shouted again, one hand reaching for the door handle.

"No, that is not true!" Laura exclaimed, but it was much too late. Elouise, tears now running down her cheeks, threw open the door and ran out, the sound of her sobs echoing down the corridor.

CHAPTER TWELVE

It had been a long and exhausting night. Laura had barely slept a wink, worrying about Elouise and fretting over both what she had seen and what she had said. At the Duke's insistence, she had left Elouise alone until the morning, allowing her to either sleep or to come to Laura's door, should she need her. However, as dawn broke and the sun began to stream towards the house, Laura felt her urgency begin to grow.

She was desperate to speak to Elouise, desperate to explain to her that what she had seen meant only that Laura and the Duke cared for one another but that it did not mean they did not care for her. She wanted to tell her that the Duke had only good things planned for her, that she would have a happy future here and that, in the end, it would be Laura who would be returning to the orphanage and leaving them both behind here.

Swallowing her tears, Laura paced up and down her bedchamber, ignoring the breakfast tray that had been brought in only a few minutes before. She didn't want to leave this place and certainly didn't want to leave the Duke, but the thought of never returning to the other girls at the orphanage, the ones who she *knew* would be waiting for her to return, was more than she could bear. She had promised them that she'd come back, had promised them all that they would not be without her for too long. There was simply nothing else she could do, knowing that she both could not and would not turn her back on them now for the sake of her own personal happiness.

The Duke, of course, had not been thrilled to know that this was how Laura was thinking, even though he seemed to understand. That kiss they had shared was one that Laura knew she would never forget, even as tears came to her eyes at the memory of it. It had been the moment when she'd felt the Duke come into her heart completely, knowing that he would never be removed. Whatever happened, Laura knew that she would always love him with everything she had. She would always love him, always have a deep, abiding affection that could never be taken away. No matter what happened and even if she never saw him again in her life, that love would linger on in her heart.

How painful it was to know that she would be separated from him for good – and by her own choice also! If there was a way to be with both the Duke and her girls then, of course, she would accept it readily, but she simply could not see a way forward for such a thing to occur. She was resigned, therefore, to simply doing her best for Elouise and then departing back to London, back to Smithfield Market and back to the orphanage. It was what she had to do.

One hour later and, thinking that Elouise must be sleeping late, Laura knocked quietly on the door, expecting to find the maid within.

The door was locked.

Frowning, she turned the door handle again, not understanding why it should be so. There had always been a key in Elouise's door but Elouise had been under strict instructions not to lock it and, thus far, had not done so. There had been no need for her to do so, given that Laura herself was just next door and the maid was required to come in and out at any given time. Laura had always trusted Elouise and had found her trust to be well given, since the girl had never done something like this before – but now, Laura realized, in her state of upset, Elouise must have chosen to lock her bedchamber door tight so that Laura could not get in.

Rapping gently, Laura let out a long breath and leaned her forehead against the door. "Elouise?" she called, quietly. "Elouise, please. You must open this door now. Come along."

There was no response.

"Elouise!" Laura called again, a little more firmly. "None of this nonsense. Open the door. There are some things we must talk about."

Again, there came no reply other than the quietness

that wrapped itself around Laura's soul. She felt herself quiver with a sudden fear, her heart beating painfully.

"Oh, Miss Smith!"

Laura turned to see Elouise's assigned maid coming towards her, a slightly pinched expression on her face.

"Do you have the key, Miss Smith?" the maid continued, without waiting for Laura to greet her. "I cannot seem to get in this morning and thought it might be because you needed her to get a bit extra sleep or some such thing."

Laura shook her head, biting her lip painfully. "No," she said after a moment. "No, I have not locked this door. I believe Elouise must have done so herself." She heard the maid's quick intake of breath and looked at her again, her stomach fluttering. "Does the housekeeper have another key?"

The maid bobbed and turned on her heel without so much as a word, her steps quick as she hurried back along the corridor in search of the housekeeper. Laura, having nothing else to do other than wait, stood quietly outside Elouise's door, knocking intermittently in the hope that Elouise would eventually decide to come and answer it. She did not know what had become of her charge, wondering if she was deliberately choosing to ignore Laura completely, simply to put fear into her heart, or whether she was somewhere in the room, curled into a tight ball as she sobbed. Either way, Laura simply wanted to get into the room so that she might be able to find Elouise, to hold her tight and say that everything she'd seen, everything she'd heard, had a simple explanation. She wanted to tell her just how much she loved her, in the same way that she loved the other girls at the orphanage, and that the Duke loved her too. She wanted to reassure her, to help her, to give her back the hope she'd lost by stumbling in on Laura and the Duke in the library last night.

Leaning her forehead against the door, Laura let out a long sigh, filled with regret.

"Elouise," she whispered, one hand pressed flat against the door. "Please just open the door, my dear. There is so much I need to talk to you about."

Silence met her ears in a deafening roar.

Tears filled Laura's eyes as she waited, her worry filling her to capacity. The hurried sound of the maid's footsteps brought her a modicum of relief, even more, the sound of keys jangling in her hand.

"This one, miss," the maid said breathlessly, holding out the keys. "This one, the housekeeper says. She's on her way up too, miss, just as soon as she gets the rest of the maids organized."

"I'm sure her presence won't be necessary," Laura replied, with more belief than she felt. "Elouise is either sleeping heavily – for she was awake in the night – or she has decided to play some silly game of 'hide and go-seek' without informing me. She has done that before!" She tried to laugh as she turned the key in the lock but felt it stick in her throat. "Here we are then."

Handing the keys back to the maid, she opened the door and stepped inside, surprised to find the room still shrouded in darkness. The heavy drapes were still over the windows and there was no fire in the grate.

Laura shivered as the cold air of the room nipped at her.

"I'd best get a fire going," the maid muttered, hurrying towards it. "The little mistress will be cold once she gets up. The poor mite must be quite exhausted!"

Carefully making her way towards the window, Laura threw back the drapes and turned, with a bright smile on her face towards the bed, preparing to greet Elouise.

The words died in her throat. The bed was empty.

Elouise was gone.

"There we go, miss."

The maid rose to her feet, wiping her hands on her apron. "A nice warm fire to keep the chill from the room. I know we're nearing summer but still, the mornings can be very....." Her words died away as she turned to see Laura staring at the empty bed, her face paling in shock. "But where is Miss Elouise?"

Laura shook her head, finding herself almost completely frozen in place.

"Where might she be?" the maid cried again, hurrying forward now and pulling back the bedsheets as though Elouise might be hiding underneath them. "She must be here somewhere."

Knowing what the maid did not, Laura closed her eyes for a moment and steadied herself. Elouise was not hiding in the room, she was certain of it. The girl had taken herself off somewhere, in fear and upset, although where that might be, she could not say.

"Go and fetch the Duke."

She looked at the maid who looked up and, after a

moment, turned and hurried out of the room, leaving Laura alone.

Walking to the bed, Laura placed her hand on it and found it cold. Elouise had not been here in some time. Moving to the other side of the room, she found a discarded nightdress and, in pulling open the wardrobe, found some of Elouise's clothes were gone. The girl had clearly decided to dress and then leave the room, locking the door tightly behind her.

"Oh, Elouise," she whispered, her heart breaking. "Where have you gone?"

"Laura?"

She turned to see the Duke enter the room. His dark hair was sticking up in all manner of directions, his eyes wild with fear.

"She's not here, Royston," Laura whispered, as he wrapped her in his arms. "I don't know what to do."

He held her close for a moment and she leaned into him, letting his strength settle her fractious thoughts.

"We'll find her," he said, softly. "Can you trust me with that, Laura?"

Looking up at him, Laura saw the expression on his face and nodded jerkily, tears spilling from her eyes. "I am just so afraid. This is my fault, Royston."

He grasped her upper arms tightly. "No," he said, firmly, his head lowering just a little so that he might look into her face a little better. "No, Laura, this is not your fault. None of this is your fault. There was nothing wrong with what we did nor what Elouise saw. I think we were both rather flustered when she appeared and perhaps I spoke a little more firmly than I ought." The fire in his eyes dimmed for a moment, regret tugging at his lips. "I did not think for one moment that she would....."

Laura let out a shuddering breath, her lips twisting with the attempt not to let her tears fall. "We have to find her, Royston."

"And we shall." His hands drifted down her arms until they caught her hands, his head lowering to press a gentle kiss to her cheek. "We will find her, Laura, I promise. Can you trust me?"

Her eyes caught his as she nodded, and their lips met for just a moment, nothing more than a whisper caught between the two of them.

"Then go and tell Alice the news," he said, gently, his breath tickling across her cheek. "I will assemble the staff and we will begin a thorough search of the grounds. Thank goodness it has not been raining and looks to be a fair day!"

Laura closed her eyes for a moment as tears spilled from her eyes, and felt the Duke's hand brush across her cheek, capturing the moisture that had landed there.

"I will not lose another child," he promised, fervently. "Now go. Find Alice and apprise her of what has happened. I will come and talk to you both once the staff has been sent out.

Seven hours later and Laura and Alice were pacing the floor of the drawing room, having just completed a thorough search of the house in its entirety, assisted by the housekeeper and maids. The footmen had been organized by the Duke and the butler, who, along with the grounds men, gardeners and stable hands, had been sent out to search the grounds. It was to be a long search, for the grounds were extensive, and Laura felt a chill of fear wash through her as she waited for news of their return.

"It has been so long already," she murmured, half to herself, "And they have still not returned with her."

Alice threw herself down into a seat, her face paler than Laura had ever seen it. "I want to help further but I just do not know what to do."

Laura nodded, feeling exactly the same way. "At least we know she is not in the house."

A deep, fearful sigh left Alice's lips as she nodded, her teeth worrying her lip. "Indeed," she muttered, passing one hand over her eyes. "Which means that she is outside somewhere and soon, it will be getting dark."

Trying not to give in to the fear that was already beginning to crowd her soul, Laura drew in a long, shuddering breath. It was by now late afternoon, for she had only discovered Elouise's disappearance at ten o' clock this morning, but she knew they still had some hours of daylight left. "I am sure Royston will find her before then," she said, with as much confidence as she could muster, unable to even consider the thought that Elouise would be outside for another night, lost to them all. "Surely, there must be news of her soon."

Alice choked back a sob, waving Laura away as she came to console her.

"I am quite all right," she murmured, trying to remain as strong as she could. "I apologize, Miss Smith, I – "

"Laura, please."

A wan smile crossed Alice's face. "Laura, then. I apologize, Laura for being such a watering pot when you are having to be so strong. That girl has become so dear to me these last few weeks that I can hardly bear to think of her out there alone. I just pray she is not injured!" Her eyes lifted to Laura's, her lips trembling. "Why did she leave, do you think? What was her reason?"

A cloud of guilt surrounded Laura. "She stumbled across me and your brother, Lady Alice. I will not try to hide the truth from you, for it will come out eventually, although I pray you will not think ill of me. I care for your brother most deeply, but I have had to refuse his urging to remain here. I do believe he will adopt Elouise."

"But why?" Lady Alice exclaimed at once, looking almost hurt. "Why would you do such a thing when you care for him?"

"Because I must," Laura replied, her throat aching. "There are twelve other girls at the orphanage who need me. I cannot simply toss them aside in favor of my own desires and longings."

There was silence for a moment or two, which was then broken by the sound of Lady Alice sighing heavily.

"You are an extraordinary young lady, Laura," she said, softly. "I would not have thought that anyone would turn down a Duke for the sake of a few orphaned girls, except that is what you are doing. You are putting their lives before your own. I think there is so much I could learn from you, Laura. I am only sorry that I will not be able to have the pleasure of your company for much longer."

"I am sorry for that too," Laura replied, honestly. "I

have found your generosity and your kindness to be truly wonderful, Lady Alice. You have done so much for Elouise in particular and I know that she –" her throat ached all the more. "She will be very happy here, as I hope you will be also."

Lady Alice was crying openly now, tears spilling down her cheeks.

"I will miss Elouise dreadfully, as I will miss you, this house and of course, the Duke himself," Laura continued, trying to get the words out and finding it increasingly difficult to do so. "But I have many wonderful memories now and, perhaps one day, we might be able to meet again. Thank you for everything you have done, Lady Alice. You have truly changed my life for the better."

Lady Alice pulled herself out of her chair and embraced Laura, who felt tears spill down her cheeks unhindered. Together, they wept as they embraced, feeling their friendship strengthen all the more.

"I shall miss you terribly," Lady Alice whispered, stepping back but keeping a hold of Laura's hand. "How sad I am that things should not be as I had hoped between yourself and my brother. He will be a lesser man without you."

Laura wept all the harder, her emotions almost tearing her apart.

"But I understand your reasons for returning," Lady Alice finished, her own voice wobbling terribly. "You have a good heart, Laura, and even though Elouise might not understand what she saw, then I know that she will soon come to realize the truth of it. This is not your fault and not your doing, so you are not to take any of the blame on yourself, as I can see you are inclined to do."

Laura nodded jerkily, her handkerchief now a sodden mess as she tried to stem the flow of tears. "Royston asked me to trust him, to trust that he will find Elouise and that is all I can do," she said, hoarsely, suddenly forced to sit down in a chair given the weakness of her limbs. "I just pray to God that they find her soon."

CHAPTER THIRTEEN

"Alice."

John walked into the drawing room to find Alice half asleep in the chair. She jerked awake and stared at him with wide eyes, before realizing who he was. Putting a finger to her lips, she pointed in the direction of the chaise longue, and it was only then that John realized Laura was lying on it, fast asleep.

"She is exhausted," Alice whispered, reaching for his hand. "Do not wake her. I had to practically force her to eat something, for she has not eaten all day and was struggling to remain standing." She looked up at him again, her eyes anxious. "She did not want to sleep, of course, but I promised to wake her the moment there was news. Is there any?"

Shaking his head, John let his eyes linger on the brandy nearby, moving to pour himself a small glass. He did not want to lose the sharpness of his mind, but he was completely exhausted and rather cold, given that it was now growing close to dusk.

"And the men?"

John sighed heavily and came to sit by his sister. "Some remained here to ensure that your needs were taken care of and so that the house did not fall into disarray. They have now gone out to search, whilst those who were outside have returned to the house, to eat and replenish themselves. I will not give up until I find her, Alice."

She pressed his hand lightly with her own. "I know you will not, John."

Agony and fear tore through him and he had to look away. This was not what he had planned, not what he had intended. He had hoped that he would find Elouise quickly and had, in fact, gone straight to the old ruin, thinking that she had gone there. But he had been wrong. The ruin had been empty and desolate, with no sign that anyone had ever been there. He had called her name until his voice was hoarse, had tramped the grounds with his men and searched for her until his entire body ached and still, she was not in his arms.

"I should have told her before now," he muttered, passing one hand over his eyes. "She should have known the moment I decided."

Alice looked up at him and he saw, for the first time, just how red-rimmed her eyes were. Clearly, his sister cared a great deal for Elouise also.

"I have been making the necessary arrangements to adopt Elouise," he explained, quietly. "I have not yet told her for I wanted to ensure that everything was in place before I did so. Perhaps that was foolish. Perhaps I should have told her the moment I decided, so that she knew my intentions. Then she might not have reacted so badly when she found Laura and me....." Trailing off, he looked away, his eyes landing on Miss Smith and finding his heart aching for her. He knew that she was to return to London soon, knew that he had to let her go, but that did not stop his heart from crying out in pain at that truth. He longed for her to stay and was almost fearful of what his life would be like without her, what Elouise's life would be like without Miss Smith by her side. He had to think of something, some way to keep her here with him. There had to be something he could say that would convince her that to remain here, to accept his proposal of marriage, without feeling as though she were letting all of her other charges down.

"She will not turn her back on the rest of the girls, John," Alice said, softly. "She cannot. She has too good a heart, even though it belongs to you."

John swallowed hard, letting his gaze drift back towards his sister. "I love her, Alice."

Alice smiled gently, despite her worry. "I think she loves you too, John, but unless you can find a way to move the orphanage up here, then I fear she will never be able to commit herself in the way she longs to do."

Silence filled the room. Silence that was broken by the sudden sound of running feet coming towards them. John and Alice jumped from their seat at the noise. Laura woke with a sudden jerk as there came a loud rap on the door, followed by the face of one of their footmen.

"George," John said quickly, beckoning him inside. "What news?"

"We have found her, your grace."

There was a gasp from both Alice and Laura as Laura hurried forward to stand beside him – and he felt her hand slip into his, her fingers twining with his own. He could not look at her but felt his heart quicken nonetheless.

"Where?" he asked, knowing that he must ask the dreaded question. "And what state is she in?"

The footman swallowed, hesitating for a moment. "She was speaking to us, your grace, but is very quiet and it can be hard to make her out. One of the men found what appears to be an old mine shaft on the edge of your estate. She has fallen into that and I would surmise that she has been unable to make her way out again."

Laura choked back a sob as Alice asked, "Is she terribly injured?"

The footman shook his head. "It is hard to say, my lady. She was speaking to us and has not said anything about a broken limb or the like, but I think it is best if you come at once, your grace. We have not yet worked out a way to get into the shaft itself, although some men have gone for sturdy rope and more torches."

"We will all come," Laura said before John could reply. "I just need my shawl."

"And mine," Alice agreed, hurrying towards the door. "We will not be a moment."

∽

The air was damp, and the grey sky filled with darkening clouds as John pulled up his horse by a cluster of trees that climbed up and over a small hill, jumping down from his mount before turning to help Alice and then Laura. The footman had ridden also and was throwing his reins over a branch before hurrying towards the trees. John followed suit, as did the ladies, before catching Laura's hand in his own and quickly moving forward.

"This way, your grace," the footman called, but John did not need his direction. He could hear the voices of the men and could see the flickering torches through the trees. He had never been to this part of his estate before, he was sure, for it was right at the border and had such thick, dense trees that it was best left alone. The ground was rough and hard, thorns tearing at his clothes as he walked. He turned to ensure that Alice was all right and saw her nod at him. His heart hammered in his chest as he drew close to the men, who all stepped aside when they saw him.

"Where is she?"

His voice was cold and rasping, fear tearing at him as one of the men pointed to a large hole that seemed to slope inwards into the hill. "In there?"

"Royston?"

Laura gasped aloud and squeezed his hand tightly, before hurrying forward to fall on her knees by the hole. "Elouise?"

"Oh, Miss Smith!"

The girl sounded as though she were crying.

"I am so sorry."

He came to stand by Miss Smith, holding onto her shoulder so that she would not tip forward. "You need not apologize, Elouise. Now stay exactly where you are. I am coming down for you."

There was no reply and Laura looked up at him frantically, her fingers digging into his arm as she got to her feet. "You cannot mean to...."

"I must," he said firmly, bending over to kiss her cheek, caring not a jot for what any of his staff would think. "She will be my daughter and so I must be the one to fetch her out."

Laura held his gaze for another moment before nodding and stepping back, her hand falling to her side. Alice came to stand with her and the ladies linked arms and held hands as John instructed the men to wrap the rope about his middle and then over his shoulders so that he would be safely secured within.

"This will take a good deal of strength," he warned, as he approached the hole. "Do be sure to hold onto me tightly."

The main gardener stepped forward to take command. "We had to do this before with a horse that got stuck in the mire," he said, addressing the men. "Wrap this rope around that large tree over there and then prepare to hold tight. Lowering won't be the hard part. It'll be getting them both back up again."

John nodded, his heart beating a little more quickly than he would like, for there was, of course, a little trepidation about what he was about to do – not that he wanted his men to know such a thing, of course.

"Here, your grace." One of the men held out a flaming torch for him to hold, which he accepted gratefully. He couldn't see a thing inside the hole at all but knew he would need to have a light in order to reach the ground safely.

"Ready?" he called, seating himself down on the very edge of the hole. "Take the strain."

The men pulled, and John felt the rope tighten about him. Taking a deep breath, he pushed himself forward with his free hand, his breath catching in his chest as he hung, suspended in the air. He heard Laura cry out as the rope dug through his shirt, rubbing against his skin.

"And lower!" he shouted, hoping that this would bring both Laura and Alice reassurance that he was all right. "Carefully now."

Gritting his teeth at the pain of the rope burning his skin, John held the torch out as he was dropped further into the mine shaft, looking all about him for Elouise. He prayed that her silence did not mean the worst, suddenly haunted by the idea that he would find her already gone from this earth – and then his torch caught the sight of someone huddling in the corner.

"Elouise," he breathed, as his feet hit solid ground. "My dear child. Come here."

The rope slackened, and he shouted up for them to stop, moving a couple of steps closer to Elouise as she tried to stand.

Holding the torch to one side, he saw her tear-streaked face as she hobbled towards him, her eyes filled with pain.

Catching her at once, he held her tightly and felt every single part of him flood with relief. She was safe. She was secure, and she was his.

"I am sorry, your grace," Elouise whispered, shuddering against him as she began to sob. "I tried to run away and I fell down this big hole and now my ankle is sore. I couldn't get out and no-one could hear me and I was so afraid...." She trailed off, her whole body shaking with sobs.

"Hush, now," he soothed, holding her tightly as he discarded the torch altogether. "We will get you out of here this very moment. Miss Smith and Lady Alice are desperate to see you."

Elouise sniffed and wiped her nose with the back of her hand. "Is Miss Smith very angry with me?"

He smiled and tugged the rope with one hand holding her tightly against him so that his men could lift them both together. "No, my dear. She is not angry in the least. Come on. Let me take you home."

Elouise clung to him as the rope pulled hard about him, tearing at his skin even more – but John barely felt it. The relief that he had Elouise safely in his arms meant more to him than anything, knowing that their horrendous ordeal was finally over. His muscles quivered as, slowly, the rope inched them both up together but his strength never so much as flickered. Soon, strong hands had wrapped themselves around his shoulders and had taken hold of Elouise, bringing them both up safely to the surface.

Letting out a long sigh of relief, John flopped back onto the grass and closed his eyes as he heard Miss Smith cry out as she held Elouise close. Both she and Elouise were crying, murmuring words to one another as the men tried their best to cut the rope that was still about him. He was completely exhausted but utterly relieved, glad to have Elouise safely back home.

"Thank you, Royston."

Miss Smith was standing by his side now and, as he rose to his feet, he took her hands in his. Elouise was with Alice, being hugged tightly as the men swarmed about them, quickly setting up a barrier around the mine shaft so that such a thing would not happen again.

"I knew I could trust you," Laura said, softly. "You brought her back to me – to us, Royston. I can never thank you enough."

He pressed one hand to her cheek and felt her lean into it, his heart both full and aching in equal measure. "Then shall we all return home, my dear? I think we all could do with a good rest."

She smiled then, her eyes damp with tears. "Yes, I think so."

"And the doctor for Elouise, I think," he said, as they turned back towards Elouise and Lady Alice. "That ankle is not broken at least, but I would like him to look over her carefully."

Bending down on his knees, he smiled in Elouise's face as she looked back at him, clearly a little uncertain.

"Elouise," he said, honestly. "I am sorry for speaking to you with such firmness last night. I was a little unsettled but, be that as it may, I will not apologize for asking you to show a little more respect to Miss Smith. That is what your life here will be like, Elouise. I will guide you and cherish you, teach you and support you – but I will not hesitate to reprimand you when you require it. Do you understand?"

Elouise nodded quickly, her eyes rounding.

"I should like you to stay here with me, Elouise," he continued, softly. "I should like to adopt you, if you will let me." He watched as Elouise glanced up at Miss Smith, a small smile tugging at the corners of her mouth. "What say you, my dear girl? Will you stay here with me, to make this place your home? Will you be my daughter and let me be your father? I know you already have a papa and that he was sadly taken from you but I will do all I can to treat you with as much love and as much devotion as he would have done."

One hand reached for his and he took it gently.

"I won't have to go back to the orphanage?"

Shaking his head, he tried to say more but found his throat closing up such was the wonder in her eyes.

"And I can stay here with you forever?"

"Forever," he promised, squeezing her hand. "What do you think?"

Two small arms wrapped around his neck as Elouise, somewhat unsteadily, stepped forward into his arms.

"Yes, please," she whispered, holding onto him tightly. "I would like that very much."

"Good," he replied, hearing Alice sniffling beside him as he fought the joyful tears that had sprung into his eyes. "Then it is settled. From this day on, you will be Lady Elouise Royston, daughter to the Duke of Royston and your home will be here with me."

She stepped back and looked into his face. "And with Miss Smith, too."

A shuddering breath caught his chest as he shook his head. "Miss Smith must return to the other girls, although I am certain she will visit whenever she can," he murmured, hating the pain that sliced through his joy. "Do you understand that, Elouise?"

Elouise looked up at Laura just as John did too, seeing the wobbly smile on her face.

"I suppose I do," she murmured, her smile fading just a little. "Although I will miss you very much, Miss Smith."

"And I will miss you too," Laura replied hoarsely, although her eyes did not once move to his. "But you will be very happy here with the Duke, won't you? It will be a truly wonderful life and you shall never be lonely again."

Elouise sighed but nodded, her arms still wrapped around John's neck. "But you will visit, Miss Smith?"

There was a momentary pause before Laura replied with an 'of course' – but John could hear the tremble in her voice. He knew that she would not often be able to visit the manor house, would not often be able to get away from the orphanage that needed her so desperately. He held Elouise tight as he rose to his feet, offering the crook of his arm to Laura, who took it at once. Even though he knew that she was to leave him, even though he knew their love could not find its own, joyful conclusion, he had to be near her for the little time he had left.

"Come, then," he murmured as Alice, torch in hand, led the way back through the trees. "Let us all return home."

"Home," Elouise sighed, happily. "And I shall never run away again."

CHAPTER FOURTEEN

One week later and Laura knew it was time to return to London. Elouise was back to her bright, happy self and with only a sprained ankle as a reminder of her troubles, she had apparently quite forgotten the very reason she had been angry with both John and Laura and was bouncing around the estate with her usual bright spirits. They had enjoyed a wonderful day together and Elouise was now fast asleep in bed whilst Laura's maid was busy packing her things. Laura, unable to be in the room whilst such a thing was occurring, had chosen to come to the library for a time and was now looking out of the window at the growing dusk, feeling her heart tear painfully at the thought of leaving the only place she'd ever really come to think of as a home.

"I am to leave come the morrow, as you know," Lady Alice murmured, coming to stand by the window alongside Laura. "Are you sure you are quite ready to join me?

You need not if you would prefer to stay here for a little longer."

Laura let out a shaky breath, knowing that despite her longing to stay. "I cannot," she whispered, hoarsely. "The girls need me."

Lady Alice nodded, her smile sad. "I knew you would say such a thing, Laura, and yet I wish there was something I could do in order to assist you in this difficult matter." A quiet laugh escaped her. "Perhaps I ought to adopt the rest so that you are freed from your obligations there."

That brought a smile to Laura's face. "I think you will do better in this life without twelve young girls hanging onto your skirts, Lady Alice! They can be a handful!"

Lady Alice laughed, her eyes sparkling. "Tell me about them."

Laura, who was glad to be able to speak of her charges, launched into a discussion about them all, telling Lady Alice about them each individually. She described not only the color of their hair and eyes but also about their different characters. One young lady, Martha, was a quiet sensitive soul and Laura found that she was more concerned about her than about any of the others, for Mary Sanders did not take to quiet, rather unobtrusive girls. She thought their silence was more foreboding than anything else and was often rather harsh with Martha.

"You know them all very well," Lady Alice murmured, gently. "They are very blessed to have your company with them, Laura."

Laura sniffed despite her determination not to cry. "I

must just hope that one day soon, I will be able to return here."

Lady Alice's face lit up.

"To visit Elouise, of course," Laura finished, seeing the disappointment shudder into every curve of Lady Alice's face. "Although I do not think that it shall be very often, I'm afraid."

Lady Alice sighed again, shaking her head. "I do not want you to go, of course, but I want to assure you that our friendship will continue long after our time here has come to an end. I will write to you very often – as often as I can – and I shall, of course, help you in any way I can, whenever I can. You must promise to ask me for help should you ever need it, Laura. I will not allow you to struggle." She raised one eyebrow and looked pointedly at Laura, who had no other recourse but to nod.

"I will."

Lady Alice smiled, turning her head to see the door open and the Duke to step inside. "I think I had best leave you now, my dear. I will see you in the morning, bright and early."

"Bright and early," Laura repeated, even though every fiber of her being felt as though it was being torn apart. She did not look round, not even when Lady Alice left the room, her breath coming quickly as the presence of the Duke filled the room. She stayed exactly where she was, her eyes fixed on nothing in particular, blood roaring in her ears.

"And so, we must say goodbye."

His voice was low and gruff, and Laura felt her eyes prick with tears.

"Yes," she whispered, sadly. "It seems we must. You will do as I ask, will you not?"

His footsteps caught her ears as he walked towards her, coming to stand directly by her side although he did not take her hand as she had expected him to.

"Yes," he said, slowly. "I will ensure that Elouise says her farewell to you and then engage her in some wonderful activity so that she will not have to wave you off. Not if you think that will be too painful for her."

Laura nodded, looking up at him gratefully. "I think it will be, yes. I appreciate your willingness in this, Royston and I confess that it would be all too painful for me also."

His lips caught in a rueful smile. "And I, my dear Laura." His expression clouded, and his fingers touched her own, sending thrills up her spine. "I feel my heart breaking even now."

Her eyes fluttered closed as he leaned down towards her, his breath whispering across her cheek before he placed his lips there, brushing them along the curve of her jaw before catching her lips. She let herself linger there for a moment but broke it sooner than she wanted to, knowing that she could not let her heart become caught up with him again. Had she not spent the last few days trying to put some sort of distance between them both? Had she not made sure not to be in his company alone all too often? It was her way of forcing herself to separate from him before she had even left the manor house.

"And yet I am happier than I have been in as many years," he murmured quietly his eyes searching hers.

"Whilst I am truly sad to be losing you, I cannot be sorry for what you have brought into my life. Elouise has become the light in my dark world and, thanks to you and your encouragement, I will not go back into the shadows again. Although," he finished, his fingers dropping from her cheek. "My life shall certainly be somewhat less without you in it."

She smiled, glad that he was not trying to convince her to stay. "I will never forget you, Royston," she promised, one hand resting lightly on his chest. "You have taken my heart and it will never belong to anyone but you. No matter how many days, how many years go by, I will always hold you here." She pressed her hand to her heart, as a tear trickled down her cheek. The Duke wiped it away with a gentle hand before bringing her into his embrace.

Laura went willingly, resting her head on his chest as he held her close. There was nothing but acceptance in their time together, a realization and an understanding that this moment was all they had left.

~

The following day, John found himself more in agony than he had ever thought possible. He had taken Elouise to say her goodbyes to Laura – or Miss Smith, as she was to her – and had found himself unable to stop looking at the lady. She was white faced, with red-rimmed eyes and dark shadows crossing her expression whenever she caught his glance, but to him, she had never looked more beautiful.

Elouise had, of course, cried at saying goodbye to Miss Smith, but a promise of a horse ride down to the old mine shaft, so they could see the progress the men were making in filling it up brought a small smile back to her face. In fact, even as they walked towards the stables, Elouise was already wiping the last of her tears away and beginning to chatter amicably about what they might find at the old mine shaft, mentioning that she would like to go and visit the old ruin again on the way back. John nodded and smiled and listened and all the while felt his heart remain with Miss Smith on board the carriage, more upset than he could say at the thought of never seeing her again.

"It will be quite quiet here without Miss Smith," Elouise mused, as they rode carefully towards the border of John's estate. "Although Lady Alice has already told me that I am to have a governess." She scrunched up her nose and looked up at John, who couldn't help but laugh. "What is a governess, Royston?"

He grinned at her. "A governess is a lady who will teach you everything you need to know in order to become a successful young lady of the realm," he explained, seeing the slight flicker of confusion in her eyes. "You have a good deal of learning ahead of you, my dear girl, but I am sure you will take to it very well."

Elouise did not look entirely convinced. "But you will still play with me, won't you?" she asked, a little doubtfully. "With Lady Alice and Miss Smith gone, I wonder if I won't be lonely."

Her sadness crept back into her expression and he attempted to buoy her at once. "Of course, I shall still play with you, and we will dine together each evening. You must remember, however, that you have lessons to take and I have business to attend to. There comes a lot of responsibilities with being a Duke." *Responsibilities I have neglected for some time,* he thought to himself a little wryly.

"And will this governess play with me?" Elouise asked, her eyes looking up at him hesitantly. "When I was at the orphanage, I always had the other girls to play with, although I didn't always want to play."

"I am sure she will," John replied, with as much certainty as he could inject into his voice. "In fact, I have yet to choose your governess, Elouise so I shall make sure that your requirements are noted and fulfilled by whomever it is I choose."

This brought a small smile to her face and she looked away, a little brighter than before.

"Now," he said, grandly. "Shall we go and see the progress the men have been making in filling up the mine shaft? And after that, we might go to the old ruin and see what we can find there!"

She beamed at him, her eyes filled with delight. "Yes, please, Royston!"

Chuckling, he led her towards the woods and, within a few minutes, they were walking towards the mine. However, something Elouise had said lingered on in his mind, something about how she had often played with the other girls. For the first time, John let his thoughts linger on each of them.

Would he have taken to each of them in the same way as he had taken to Elouise, had they appeared instead of her? Were they not equally as alone as she was? Did they not all deserve a good home?

His brow furrowed as the men welcomed Elouise and began to show her the work they had been doing. Would not all of those girls have brought light back to his life, had they come to his home with Miss Smith? Elouise was fortunate indeed to have been chosen but it would be just himself, Elouise and the rest of his staff living in this large manor house for some years to come. After all, Alice was to find herself an appropriate husband this Season, once, of course, he had been given the opportunity to look into the particular gentleman, whoever he was to be, but that meant that she would not be returning to Royston manor in the near future, if at all. A betrothal usually lasted less than a month, which meant that Alice could easily be married by the end of the Season and life would change for him all over again. He would have a brother in law. Perhaps nephews and nieces one day, but there would only ever be himself and Elouise living in this house alone.

"Unless....."

The idea came to him in a flash and he almost dismissed it out of hand, given the sheer ridiculousness of it. But, taking in a breath, he let it settle for a moment or two, beginning to think through it all. It was a little ridiculous, yes, but it would make both Elouise and him happy, as well as bringing joy to Miss Smith, should it all work out. He would need to make an inordinate number of arrangements, for there would be a good deal to put in place and, of course, he would be the talk of all of England – but that did not dissuade him in any way. He was a Duke, after all, which meant that he could do the most provocative things he wished and would not bat an eyelid about what others thought. There would be no fall from grace for him, for he was the highest titled gentleman in all of England, save for the King himself.

His eyes caught Elouise's as she laughed at something one of the men said, feeling his heart lift with happiness as she smiled at him. This was a foolish idea admittedly but, regardless, he was going to consider it further and then begin to put everything into place. It would take a few weeks to have everything organized but then, once it was all done, he could finally make a trip to London and explain it all to his dear Laura. They would not be separated for long and, should it all work out to his satisfaction, they would not be separated again.

CHAPTER FIFTEEN

The carriage rolled through the cobbled London streets and Laura felt her heart sink all the lower. Yes, she was looking forward to seeing the girls again, but she was farther than ever from the Duke and Elouise.

"Here we are," Lady Alice said, softly. "I confess, my dear girl, that I do not want to be parted from you, but that time has now come." Reaching forward, she pressed Laura's hands for a moment. "You have become a very dear friend to me and this is not to be goodbye. We shall see each other again, very soon."

Laura tried to smile but found that she could not. Despite Lady Alice's assurances, she felt spirits sink all the lower, knowing that soon Lady Alice would be caught up in society's whirlwind and unable to spare even a moment to call upon the orphanage.

"May I wish you the very best with your search for a suitable gentleman," she said, a little dully. "I pray it is successful."

Lady Alice blushed. "Thank you, Laura. I am sure it will be. Elouise will have a new uncle very soon."

Swallowing her sob, Laura turned towards the open door of the carriage and, with a final squeeze of Lady Alice's hand, stepped out of the carriage door and looked up at the old, dirty building of the orphanage.

"Thank you for all of your kindness, Lady Alice," she said, turning away from it. "Should you wish to write to me, you know where I will be." She said this with only a small flicker of hope but Lady Alice nodded fervently.

"Of course I will," Lady Alice said, hastily, leaning out of the carriage after her. "I do not want our friendship to come to a close, Laura, even though you may think so. I will not be tossed about by all manner of things within society but, instead, shall ensure that I keep my wits about me and remind myself that what matters most is the state of one's heart." She smiled at Laura, her eyes filling. "I have learned that from you. To have kindness, compassion, and love in one's heart is better than anything on the outside. You are my inspiration, my dear friend, and do not think for one moment that I intend to forget you." A single tear slid down her cheek, landing on the cobblestones below the carriage. "I shall write just as often as I can."

Now believing that Lady Alice would do just as she said, Laura felt her own tears come in earnest. "Thank you, Lady Alice," she said, hoarsely. "I will reply to you when I can, of course."

"Good." Picking up her reticule, Lady Alice pulled something out of her bag and handed it to Laura. It was money. A good deal of money.

Laura shook her head. "No, Lady Alice, I cannot take this."

"Yes, you can," Lady Alice said, firmly. "And you will. If not to spend on yourself, then to spend on your girls. You must take care of both yourself and them. I will send you some more next quarter. Be sure of it."

Laura wanted to refuse, wanted to say no but in her mind's eye, saw the new clothes she could buy the girls, the decent food she might be able to purchase once in a while, under Mary Sander's nose.

"Thank you, Lady Alice," she whispered, looking up at her friend. "I know the girls here will appreciate this."

Lady Alice smiled, looking relieved. "You are more than welcome, my dear. Write to me soon. I will miss your company."

That said, the door was closed, the horses moved, and the carriage rolled away, carrying Lady Alice with it. Laura waved as she watched, hating to see it move away and carry so many of her memories with it.

Turning back to the orphanage, she looked down at her bags and, with a heavy sigh, picked them up as best she could before staggering towards the house. This was the life she had to become used to again. There would be no more footmen to aid her with such things, no maids to come with trays of tea, cakes, and biscuits. Instead, she would have to be all things to all people, doing all she could to keep the girls as happy and as content as could be.

. . .

CHAPTER 15

One step inside the orphanage told her that all was not well.

The place was deathly silent, her footsteps echoing on the creaky wooden floor.

"Hello?" she called, wandering towards the kitchen and hoping the cook was there. "Hello? Mary? Helen?"

There came no answer. Peeking around the kitchen door, she saw the cook hard at work, busy chopping onions or something similar.

"Ah, cook, good to see you," she exclaimed, hurrying forward. "how have you been since I went away?"

The cook looked up and Laura saw that her face was pale with bloodshot eyes.

"Glory be," the cook whispered, putting the knife down and coming towards Laura. "Glory be, it is you."

She caught Laura's hands and held them tightly, her eyes filling with bright, shining tears. "Oh, it's just been terrible, Miss Laura. I was praying and praying you'd come back here."

Laura's gut wrenched as the cook urged her to sit down, still holding her hands all the while.

"Where are the girls?" Laura asked, hoarsely, wondering why it was all so quiet. "Where have they gone?"

"They'll be back afore long," the cook said, getting up from her chair. "Miss Sanders has started taking them to Smithfield Market, down the far end nearer to the gentry." She twisted her lips, her displeasure evident. "They've got to sell their own wares now and look as sad as possible in doing it."

Laura caught her breath, her eyes widening. "What?"

she whispered, as the cook bustled about. "But the girls always did their embroidery and the like here, and then Mary would sell it herself. Why has she taken them to the streets?"

The cook shook her head, lifting the corner of her apron to wipe at her eyes before handing Laura a cup with a small chip and then setting the teapot and milk jug on the roughhewn table. "She thought they might be able to make a little bit more money, what with their sad eyes and sorry tales." She sat back down and continued to cut up the potatoes. "And she was right. You should see the new hat she's bought herself."

Laura could hardly take this in, her breath catching in her chest as she stared at the cook, wanting it all desperately to be some kind of dream.

"I should have come back sooner."

The cook shook her head. "This ain't your fault, Miss Laura. None of it is. It's all that Mary Sanders, and well you know it."

"But what about Helen?" Laura asked, desperately. "She was always a good sort, able to understand what the girls needed. I thought she'd do awfully well."

A long, heavy sigh escaped the cook. "Helen's a foolish girl. As soon as Miss Sanders realized that Helen wasn't about to do what she wanted, she managed to find her another position. A *better* position in fact, so that no-one could say that Mary Sanders didn't take care of her staff." She lifted one eyebrow in Laura's direction. "But, of course, if that had been you, you'd have seen what Miss Sanders was up to and would have refused to go – but that ain't Helen. She saw the money and saw the house and agreed almost at once! Them girls have been on their own ever since."

Laura sipped her tea and tried to think carefully. "What has Mary been doing?"

"All sorts," the cook replied, hacking at the potatoes with a little more force than was needed. "Getting them to stay up all hours to get as much embroidery done as possible. Doesn't seem to notice when they miss meals and if one of them gets caught crying about something or other, they're given a sharp slap and warned to keep their tears for the streets." She grimaced and shook her head, her eyes narrowing. "There's been many a girl coming back from selling their wares with red-rimmed eyes and tear-stained cheeks – but with all their embroidery gone. Miss Sanders can see that it works, too. That's why she's keeping on doing it."

Laura took in a breath and let it shudder out of her, trying her best to think calmly.

"I ain't saying that Miss Sanders is thinking of getting rid of you too, Miss Laura, but I'd be careful around her," the cook finished, looking at her carefully. "She's a changed woman, that Miss Sanders, that's for sure, but those girls need you, Miss Laura. They need you more than ever before."

"I'm glad I came back," Laura whispered, half to herself. "My poor, poor girls."

∼

Two hours later and Laura walked into the girls' shared bedroom, her eyes taking in each and every face. The girls, as one, rose to their feet with clamoring voices, all trying to get near her at once. Tears flowed down almost every face as Laura embraced them all, one at a time, taking in their pale cheeks, their sorrowful eyes, their dull, tired expressions.

"Elouise is going to stay with the Duke," she explained when the girls looked at her expectantly. "He is adopting her."

There wasn't even a hint of jealousy as the girls expressed their delight that Elouise would have a happier life than she had ever had here. They had all known – and sympathized – with just how upset she had been.

"I am sorry to hear that Miss Sanders has been treating you so badly," Laura said gently, brushing the blonde hair out of Mary's face, the youngest child at the orphanage at only three years of age. "You have not *all* had to go out, have you?"

The eldest girl, Betty, who was twelve, nodded her head. "I've had Mary and Rosemary to take care of, Miss Laura," she explained, talking about the two youngest girls. "They stand with me and help sell whatever we have."

Laura closed her eyes for a moment, feeling a spurt of anger race through her. "That won't be happening any longer, I promise. Things will go back to how they were before."

Unfortunately, that did not bring a smile to any of the girl's faces.

"I ain't so sure Miss Sanders will like that idea, Miss Laura," Betty said, slowly. "She's treated us different these last few weeks and seems to be enjoying it too. I don't think she's going to want to give it all up just because you say so."

Laura knew that she was only in Miss Sanders's employ and that she did not have any particular clout, but neither could she just let Miss Sanders continue to treat the girls in such a disgraceful way. They deserved the best life that they could have, even in an orphanage, and that didn't mean standing on street corners trying to flog their wares.

"Don't worry," she promised, seeing a flare of hope in Betty's eyes. "I'll think of something. I have arranged to speak to Miss Sanders this evening and, hopefully, by then, I'll have something in mind to put a stop to all of this. I just need you to trust me."

The girls nodded, smiles appearing on some small faces. Their trust in her brought an ache to her heart as well as a growing frustration that she could not do more for them.

"I will think of something," she whispered again, before hugging the girls close once more.

CHAPTER SIXTEEN

"Come in."

Laura took a deep breath and opened the door, praying silently that her ruse would work.

"Ah, Laura," Mary Sanders cooed, not looking in the least bit glad to see her. "Do come in. Sit down. I suppose you are tired from your trip back to London but I'm afraid I can't spare you even an extra hour or two of rest. You will need to go straight back into your duties."

Laura sat down opposite Mary Sanders, taking in the new gown that she wore with a suspicious eye.

"And how does little Elouise do?" Mary Sanders continued, not really looking Laura in the eye but rather looking past her, as though she did not particularly care about the girl whatsoever. "Settled with the Duke, is she? I am glad, of course."

"Why are you glad, Mary?"

The question seemed to startle Mary Sanders, who frowned almost immediately, her eyes finally fixing on Laura.

CHAPTER 16

"There is no need to take a particular tone with me, Miss Laura," she said, firmly, her gaze direct as she lifted her chin a notch. "I am glad for Elouise, of course."

Laura did not back down, her fingers curling into a fist such was her anger. "Are you glad because the Duke was able to give such a wonderful financial gift to the orphanage?" she asked, narrowing her eyes. "Or is it that you are truly delighted that Elouise is finally getting a new home instead of being forced to remain here?"

Mary Sanders looked a little stunned, clearly befuddled by Laura's angry response. "I – I am glad for both, of course."

One of Laura's eyebrows arched high. "I hardly believe that, Mary. I know you very well, remember? I know that you have always cared more about money and income than you have about the girls. That is why I was so very reluctant to leave this place, given the fact that it would be *you* that would be left behind to run this place alone. I hear Helen tried to do what she could for them, but you found her another position so that she would not bother you any longer!"

Two spots of dark red appeared in Mary's cheeks. "Don't you dare speak to me in such a way, Laura! You have no right – "

"You are treating these girls as if they are your own personal servants!" Laura interrupted, angrily. "Keeping them up all hours to work on their embroidery and the like, simply so that you may sell it? Is the orphanage in truly such a poor state that they are forced out onto the streets to sell whatever they can?"

Mary Sanders glared at her. "The orphanage costs money to run, Laura."

"Even after that generous financial gift from the Duke?"

That seemed to shut Mary up, for she struggled to speak for a moment or two, her mouth opening and shutting like a fish. Laura shook her head, her disdain growing by the minute.

"These girls are exhausted, Mary," she continued, firmly. "This nonsense is to come to an end; do you hear me?" Leaning forward in her chair, she fixed her employee with a grim stare. "The youngest, Mary, is so tired she can barely eat, such is her exhaustion. The others are more worried about her than you seem to be! How can you treat them in such an appalling manner, Mary?"

Mary Sanders swallowed hard, her cheeks now a little pale although it seemed she was attempting to find some kind of firm response that would set Laura in her place.

"I have returned now, and I will not have them treated so any longer," Laura finished, directly. "Tomorrow, the girls are to rest for as long as they please and do nothing more than eat and sleep. No more being dragged out to the streets with instructions to cry and wail and act out their grief, Mary. This has gone on long enough."

"How dare you?"

Laura's back stiffened but she forced herself to keep a hold on her temper.

"How *dare* you?" Mary hissed again, slamming one hand down hard on her desk. "You think that you can speak to me in such a way without any kind of consequences, Laura? You are nothing more than a hired worker, someone who I can let go without reason or explanation. I have nothing more to say to you. Your time here is at an end." She narrowed her eyes, leaning over the desk. "This is *my* orphanage, Laura, and it seems you have forgotten that. Now pick up your things and be on your way. You are to leave my premises tonight."

Having expected as much, Laura rose to her feet but did not move towards the door. Instead, she held out a note to Mary Sanders, who sank back down into her chair and looked at it doubtfully.

"I suggest," Laura said, calmly, praying that Mary Sanders would be taken in by her deception, "that you read this before you make any kind of decision, Mary."

For a moment, Laura thought that Mary would rip up the note and throw it in the fire without so much as looking at it but, after a tense moment, she took it carefully from Laura's fingers and opened it.

Laura sat down primly, feeling the roll of money in her pocket. A small smile tugged at her lips, but she suppressed it with an effort.

"This cannot be true," Mary whispered, her face now a deathly pale as she raised small, frightened eyes towards Laura. "This is a deception."

"Is it?" Laura stood up again and smiled down at Mary sardonically. "You are very mistrusting, Mary. Can you not understand the Duke's concern for the place where his new daughter has come from? Can you not understand that Elouise herself has told him everything about this place?"

Mary Sanders trembled visibly.

"I am, of course, in the Duke's debt for his kindness towards me. In fact," Laura continued, firmly. "Lady Alice herself considers me a friend and we are to remain in close correspondence. She intends to visit the orphanage whenever she can, for she is in London for the Season and has assured me that she will call upon me whenever she can. She herself is quite taken with Elouise and considers her to be a part of the family. I can assure you, Mary Sanders, that none of this is any kind of deception."

Aside from the note, which you pored over for hours in an attempt to make it look and sound like Royston's writing, she thought to herself, remaining exactly where she was.

Mary Sanders shook her head, looking down at the note. Laura could remember almost every word she had written, for she had read it over and over again to ensure that it sounded completely genuine. The handwriting had taken a good deal longer to perfect but perfect it she had and now, it seemed, Mary Sanders was quite taken in by it.

"He says that he wishes to have a quarterly report from you," Mary whispered, the note shaking in her hand. "A report that will detail what the girls have been doing and goes into detail about their welfare. Lady Alice will be visiting on occasion also....." She trailed off, looking up at Laura seemingly unable to get out of her chair. "Are they to become benefactors?"

Laura smiled and tugged the money out of her pocket, holding it up so that Mary Sanders could see it. "*I* am to delegate this money responsibly, as you can see from the note," she said, quietly. "So yes, Mary, it does seem as though they are to be our benefactors, but they do not trust you to delegate the money carefully nor treat these girls with the respect and consideration they deserve."

"But how could they suggest such a thing?" Mary replied, her voice breaking with suppressed emotion. "What was it you said, Laura? What did Elouise say?"

Laura snorted and walked towards the door. "I hardly think that matters, Mary, do you? Needless to say, the Duke will be keeping a very close eye on this establishment and you do not want to displease a Duke of the realm now, do you? His displeasure will become known all throughout London, if not England as a whole, and you will find your reputation somewhat sullied."

Her reputation was of great importance to Mary Sanders, Laura knew and smiled to herself as she saw the lady shrink back into her chair.

"Now," she finished, opening the door. "Am I still to go and collect my things? Or have you had a change of heart?" She held the money up again for another moment, ensuring Mary's eyes landed on it before pocketing it again carefully.

"Go," Mary snarled, suddenly furious with the way this had been foisted upon her. "Go back to your rooms and do whatever you wish, Laura. It seems I have no other choice but to bow to you, since the Duke has decided to favor you and not me. I regret ever allowing you to go with him!"

Laura chuckled and pulled the door open, a sense of

satisfaction filling her. "I'm afraid it is much too late for all that, Mary," she said, shrugging as Laura looked back at her employer. "Now, do excuse me whilst I go and tell the girls that they are to do nothing but rest tomorrow. I am sure they will be very glad to hear it."

And so saying, she sailed through the door, filled with nothing more than satisfaction and delight.

CHAPTER SEVENTEEN

"'Of course, I am glad to be the orphanage's benefactor,'" Laura read aloud, a small smile on her face. "'I cannot abide the thought of those girls being treated in such a manner and shall make sure to write to Mary Sanders myself, so that she is aware that I am in league with you! You are very clever to have come up with such a scheme and I am truly glad that you wrote to me to seek my help. It is, after all, what I begged you to do and now I feel as though I am able to help those lesser than myself, which is something I am most glad of.'"

Laura smiled to herself, feeling happier than ever that Lady Alice had been so willing to go along with Laura's scheme. She had written to her the day after her conversation with Mary Sanders, recalling that Lady Alice had begged her to ask her for help should she require it – and require it, she had done! The letter continued, and she continued to speak it aloud to the empty kitchen whilst her cup of tea grew cold on the table. "'I have, of course, written to my brother to inform him of what you have done. I do not want you to be angry with me about that, for you know as well as I that he will wish to know all about it. I am quite certain that he will be glad to know of your progress.'"

Her stomach tightened for a moment as Laura allowed her thoughts to drift back towards the Duke. It was almost inevitable that Lady Alice should mention him in her reply, but Laura had not been prepared for the depth of feeling that hit her as she returned her mind to him. She had not thought of him in some days, having had her mind entirely caught up with the tense atmosphere between herself and Mary Sanders, although she was glad that the girls had been able to return to their much quieter life these last few days. That very evening, when she had gone to speak to them all with reassurance and hope, she had seen the sheer relief on their faces as she had spoken and had been required to comfort a few of them for a long time, hating that they had been so lost and alone without her.

Reading the last paragraph of Lady Alice's letter, Laura laughed softly as she heard of Lady Alice's difficulties in choosing between one of two particular gentlemen. They both, by all appearances, seemed to be very well suited to her, but she could not make her mind up about which one was best. She did mention that one stirred more feeling in her heart than the other and stated that she wished that she had such strength of feeling as both Laura and her brother had, which made Laura sigh quietly to herself. Sometimes, she thought it might be best for Lady Alice *not* to have such intense feelings as the ones she experienced for Royston, for then she would never experience such pain and such struggle as Laura now endured. But, then again, such feelings were, in fact, truly wonderful and she could not imagine never experiencing them in her life.

"Miss Laura?"

Turning around in her seat, Laura saw the cook bustling into the kitchen, her eyes bright with excitement.

"Yes?" Laura asked, folding up the letter and pocketing it. "What's the matter?"

"Elouise is here!"

Laura stopped dead as she rose from her chair, frozen in place for a moment.

"With the Duke!" the cook exclaimed, setting down her tray of fresh fruit and vegetables. "And they're asking for you, Miss Laura."

Something like ice filled her veins, rushing all through her, followed by a burning, searing heat. She could barely breathe, having to lean heavily on the table for a moment as she struggled to drag in air. Shivers were running all through her, sending weakness into her legs and arms. The Duke was here? With Elouise? Why?

"Come now!" the cook exclaimed, looking concerned as she came to Laura's side. "What's taking you so long, Miss Laura? Don't you want to see Elouise again?"

"Tell me," Laura breathed, hanging onto the cook's arm with tight, tense fingers. "Is Elouise happy? Is she content?"

A look of understanding passed over the cook's face. "He's not here to return her, if that's what you think," she said, fondly, patting Laura's shoulder. "No, quite the opposite I think. Came to see his sister, I heard him say, and wanted to see you whilst he was here." She chuckled as Laura's hand loosened on her arm. "It gave me a right laugh seeing Mary Sanders practically bowing and scraping before him. She got quite the fright to see the carriage pull up!"

Suddenly filled with urgency, Laura forced herself to hurry as she made her way towards the front of the orphanage, her hands smoothing down the front of her dress as she hurried – only to realize that she was still wearing her apron. Flushing pink, she quickly untied it and hung it over a nearby chair, before checking that her hair was as neat and as tidy as it could be. She was as plain as could be in her straight, grey dress and hair in a bun, which was just as she had appeared to the Duke on her first arrival at his home. How would he look? Would he be the same as before? It had only been a fortnight since she had left the estate but something in her was fearful that he had been dragged back into his darkness and that this was why he had returned to the orphanage.

Butterflies beat wildly in her belly as she stepped outside, delighted to see Elouise surrounded by the other girls. She looked beautiful, with a healthy glow in her cheeks and a brightness in her eyes that brought joy to Laura's heart. On seeing her, Elouise shrieked aloud and ran towards her, throwing her arms around Laura's waist.

Laura cried with happiness on seeing her, tears slipping down her cheeks as she held Elouise tightly, surrounded by the rest of the orphanage girls.

"Oh, my dear Elouise," she exclaimed, quickly wiping away her tears. "How good to see you! You look wonderful. Have you been having a grand time at the

Royston estate?" She did not dare look about her for the Duke, keeping her gaze fixed on Elouise.

Elouise nodded happily, chasing away any lingering fears in Laura's soul that Elouise had become miserable by herself in the Duke's home.

"Royston says I am to have a governess soon," she said, with a wrinkle of displeasure on her nose. "So, I cannot spend as much time playing as I would like. That is not for another month, however."

Laughing at how well-spoken Elouise had become, Laura squeezed her shoulder gently. "It will be very good for you, I'm sure." Tipping her head, she smiled down at Elouise. "And did you come to London to see Lady Alice?"

"No," Elouise replied, with a slight look of confusion. "We came to see you, Miss Smith. Why? Did you not know?"

Laura made to answer but her throat had constricted so tightly that she could not get a word out. The other girls began to chatter with Elouise again and the question was left unanswered and forgotten. Laura watched them all fondly, her two worlds coming together as one for a short time.

"Ah, Miss Smith."

Her eyes closed for a moment as she drew in a breath. He was here. He was calling her.

Turning around, she saw the Duke striding towards her, a sheaf of papers tucked under his arm. His eyes were fixed on her, his lips curving into a warm smile.

"Miss Smith," he said again, bowing formally. "It is

very good to see you again. I wonder, might I have a word with you for a moment?"

She was nonplussed by his formal attitude but then, over his shoulder, spotted Mary Sanders looking at her with such a fear on her face that Laura understood at once – and something died inside her. The Duke had not come to see *her,* as she had been led to believe but had come to see her and the girls, in order to keep up the ruse that Laura had begun with Mary Sanders. Lady Alice must have written to him very quickly, she realized, although he must have jumped in the carriage almost the moment he had received her letter.

Giving him an understanding smile, she held out one hand towards the front door. "Of course, your grace," she said, as calmly as she could. "There is a small parlor next to Mary Sanders's office where I would be glad to speak to you."

His wide grin sent her heart soaring although she tempered it with an effort.

"This way," she said, walking towards it and leaving him to follow behind.

With every step, she was more and more aware of him. Her heart was thundering wildly even though she tried to keep herself thinking rationally and calmly, telling herself over and over that this was just a discussion about what she had started with Mary Sanders. He wanted to reassure her that he would do what he could, simply out of the kindness of his own heart.

"In here, please, your grace," she murmured, pushing the door open and letting him walk through ahead of her.

Drawing in another long breath, Laura settled her shoulders and walked on through.

The moment the door was closed tightly behind her, Laura turned to see the Duke pulling at the drapes, as though ensuring they would not be seen. Frowning, she saw him set down the papers carefully on the table before stepping towards her. Her breath caught as he looked down into her eyes, no words being spoken between them.

"Laura," he whispered – and then pulled her into his arms. Strong hands caught her waist, his lips were searching for her own and she could do nothing but respond.

His kiss was swift and fierce, sending her heart racing as he held her tightly as though he would never let her go. She both loved and hated it all at once, knowing that she ought not to be allowing herself to do anything of the sort, not when she was soon to lose him all over again but finding that she could not refuse him. His lips tore from hers as he embraced her tightly, whispering words of love into her ear that sent tears into her eyes.

"Oh, my dear," he whispered, kissing her cheek. "You cannot know just how much I have missed you."

She swallowed hard, trying to keep her tears and frustration at bay.

"You still feel the same for me as you did then," he murmured, his thumb capturing her chin and lifting it just a little so that she looked into his eyes. "You still care for me, do you not?"

"Of course I do," she whispered, her heart breaking as

wretchedness filled her. "I can do nothing but love you, Royston."

"Then why do you look so miserable, my love?" he asked, tenderly. "Are you not glad to see me?"

Closing her eyes, Laura stopped more tears from falling with an effort. "You cannot know the pain and the joy that is sweeping through me at this very moment, Royston. I am delighted to be with you once again, but I am already sorrowful at the thought of having to see you leave my side once again. It is a wonderful delight and an agonizing pain all at once."

There was a short silence and Laura had to drop her gaze such was the intensity of his eyes. He was looking at her with such love, such tenderness, that she felt her heart fill with longing all over again. The same longing that had come to her when he had first kissed her at Royston manor, the same longing that she had been battling against for so long.

"I have felt the loss of your presence by my side at Royston manor," he said, honestly. "I have missed you terribly, my dear."

She smiled at him, despite the quivering within her.

"Elouise has missed you also. She has missed all the other girls at the orphanage too and has spent many evenings telling me all about them." He chuckled softly. "I believe I know each of them individually, from Mary – the youngest – to Betty, the eldest." His eyes searched hers, making her smile. "Elouise has been a little lonely without your company, Laura, as have I."

Her heart was full and breaking at the same time and, despite knowing she ought not to, her fingers twined into his shirt as she held onto him tightly. Even if it was but for a few minutes, it was worth it to her.

"Laura, I want you to come back with me."

Her eyes shot up to his and heat rushed up her spine.

"Before you say you cannot, before you say that these young girls need you, let me tell you that I know this to be the case already," he continued, halting her immediate protest. "I have heard a good deal from my sister."

She frowned as he let her out of his embrace, taking her hand to seat her down in a chair by the fire. "Lady Alice," she said quietly, realizing that what she had thought was quite right. "Yes, of course. She said that she was to write to you."

Now it was the Duke's turn to frown. "To write to me? I did not receive any such letter from her, although I did call upon her earlier this afternoon where she informed me about your previous correspondence with her. I must say, I am truly shocked by the behavior of Mary Sanders, which I have made particularly clear to her."

"And I am grateful to you for your willingness to continue with this façade for the time being," Laura said, quickly. "I know that Lady Alice was also as willing to become a supposed benefactor of this establishment and that in itself is such a blessing. I have been able to prevent Mary Sanders from continuing with her terrible exploitation of the girls and I am delighted to report that they are, on the whole, doing a great deal better."

She finished this monologue with a growing awareness that the Duke was looking at her with a good deal of confusion. She could not quite work out *what* it was she had said that confused him so much and thus remained silent, trying to make sense of it in her mind.

"My dear Laura," the Duke said slowly, one hand reaching to take hers. "I have very little idea of what it is you are talking about. I did not see Lady Alice for long, I confess, for we only stopped for an hour or so before coming here. She told me about Mary Sanders and her treatment of the girls and what you had done to mitigate it, but I had not understood that you were required to report to me any of these things!" A smile tugged at his lips. "However, I will not be continuing with any such 'façade' as you put it, for I feel there is no need."

"No need?" Laura whispered, tugging her hand from his and staring into his eyes with a sudden wave of concern. "What do you mean, no need? These girls must be protected! I cannot allow – "

The Duke cut off her words by leaning forward and planting another kiss to her lips. She was so astonished that she forgot her worry and frustration, her eyes closing tightly for a moment.

"I think that, before we continue any further with this conversation, you had best look at that pile of papers over there," the Duke murmured gently. "I mean it when I say I have every intention of taking you from this place and returning you to where I know you belong."

She sucked in a breath at the promise in his eyes.

"Back to Royston manor, which is your home," he finished, softly. There was a moment of silence before he leaned back and indicated the pile of papers. "Please, Laura. Go and look."

She did not know what else to do other than obey,

finding herself more and more puzzled by his behavior. First, he kissed her, told her he wanted her to come back with him, then said he would not aid the girls any further by continuing as the supposed benefactor she needed! Now he was telling her to look through some papers, as though everything would make sense.

Carefully, she lifted the papers up as one and brought them over to where she had been sitting. Placing them on her lap, she looked up at the Duke once more and saw him smiling at her, a spark of happiness in his eyes that went straight into her soul.

Dropping her gaze, she picked up the first sheet and saw Betty's name written there, the oldest of the orphanage girls. Confused, she read a little further, only for her heart to slam into her chest before coming to a halt completely. She could hardly breathe, her lungs screaming for air as she leafed through the papers one at a time. There were twelve sheets of paper for the twelve girls who resided at the orphanage.

"I can hardly believe this," she breathed, tears pooling in her eyes. "You are to adopt *all* of them?"

He shrugged. "Royston manor is large enough for them all, do you not think?"

She read through the names one more time, the papers shaking in her hands. "You are to take them all back with you?"

The Duke chuckled. "Of course! I realized, my love, that after you left I could not be without you. Nor could Elouise. She missed you so very much, and I could see that pain in her eyes when she spoke of you. It was a pain that resounded in my own heart that intensified with almost every hour that passed. My love, I want you to return with me to Royston manor along with all the girls that you so dearly love. They will have their home there with me and, of course, you shall take as much care of them there as you would have here."

It was more than she had ever hoped for. Setting the papers down carefully, she practically threw herself at him, her arms encircling his neck as she held onto him tightly. Half laughing, half crying, she hugged him close, hearing his chest rumble with glad laughter as he pulled her to him. Her heart was full, her joy complete. This was the most wonderful moment of her life.

"But wait," Royston said, still chuckling. "I have more to tell you."

Her eyes shining, Laura kept her hands in his.

"The cook has, of course, agreed to come with me – although I gave her strict instructions not to say a word to you when she went to fetch you!" His grin grew all the wider as she clapped one hand to her mouth. "There is a smaller kitchen and dining room in the east end of the house and I think, given that my own current cook may not take kindly to having another twelve mouths to feed without adequate warning, I thought to take back another cook who is well used to dealing with these girls."

Laura laughed and shook her head, hardly able to believe it.

"It seems you have thought of everything, Royston," she breathed, her world suddenly filled with light and color. "The girls will be so glad to be with their own cook. She knows just what to feed them and does marvelously well with so little food....although I doubt that will be the case with you, given your generous heart."

His finger trailed down her cheek, making her blush. "You have such a trust in me, my dear lady. Yes, they will be like my own children. I have always longed for a house full of children, even though that is not something that many Dukes wish for, by all accounts!" Tilting his head just a little, he let his smile linger. "Be that as it may, I will have what I desire most of all – a life filled with love, where you are by my side."

Swallowing her tears, Laura threw her arms around his neck yet again, only to be caught by a sudden thought.

"But what of Mary Sanders?" she asked, leaning back out of his embrace. "If the girls leave the orphanage, then she will simply have to find more to come and fill it. I cannot allow her to treat them in the way she has treated these girls."

"Always so tender-hearted," he murmured, gently. "You are quite right to be concerned, my dear, for Mary Sanders is *not* the kind of lady who should be running any orphanage." His expression grew a little darker as he grimaced. "The love of money is all that she cares about. It consumes her, in fact, for it is all that she thinks of. That is why she forced those girls to live in such a way. Therefore, I have informed her that I have bought the orphanage outright, giving her a fair sum in the process."

Her mind scrambled to accept what this meant.

"She will have no need to run an orphanage anywhere, my love," the Duke finished, gently. "She will have enough to live modestly until the end of her days which, I believe, she fully intends to do. I will not pretend that giving such a greedy, conniving woman additional funds was something I was particularly pleased about, but I preferred it to allowing her to set up another establishment such as this."

"I could not agree more," Laura replied, hoarsely. "Oh, Royston, is this really true?"

He pressed a kiss to her cheek. "It is," he murmured. "I could not be without you, my love, and this idea seemed to bring all the pieces of my life together again." Holding her again for another moment, he drew in a breath and let it out again before smiling broadly.

"Now," he said, a little more briskly. "You are to come with myself and Elouise as we return to Lady Alice's townhouse for dinner. You are also to reside with us overnight before we return to Royston manor in the morning."

Laura felt her heart flutter with excitement. "And the girls?"

He chuckled. "I have purloined a few of my sister's maids to assist them in their preparations for tomorrow, and have had to hire additional carriages, horses and tigers with which to drive them all back to the manor!" Gently, he brushed his fingers along her cheek. "You need not worry, my dear, they will all be quite safe and ready to leave with us tomorrow. Mary Sanders is to quit the house and the grounds by this evening and my steward, Mr. Franks, will be here to oversee things. You see? It will all come together, just as it should."

Her heart was beating with such overwhelming joy that for a moment, she was entirely robbed of speech. Her love for Royston was burning with such a strong, passionate fire that she could feel it searing through her veins, filling every part of her with joy.

"Shall you come with me, my love?"

Without hesitating, she took his offered arm and clung to him, her eyes fixed to his. "Of course I will, Royston," she whispered, happily. "I do love you so very much."

His lips brushed her gently. "And I love you, my dear Laura. I am already looking forward to taking you home."

CHAPTER EIGHTEEN

"*John!*"

Turning, John chuckled as he saw his sister hurry into the drawing room, clearly delighted to see him.

"Alice," he smiled, feeling happier than he's ever thought possible. "Everything has gone wonderfully."

She clapped her hands together before embracing him. "Oh, John. I am so happy for you. I always knew she would say yes."

He cleared his throat, feeling a little awkward all of a sudden. "Actually," he said, his eyes darting from place to place. "I did not quite ask her."

Alice's mouth dropped open, her smile fading. "John! What on earth were you thinking?"

"I fully intend to do so," he protested, raising his hands. "She was just so astonished that I thought should I say any more, she might collapse in a faint!"

"You cannot simply bring her back to the Royston's estate without at the *very* least being betrothed," Alice said, firmly. "I will not allow it, John."

Laughing at her insistence, John sat down in a seat and encouraged his sister to sit with him. "Alice, I have every intention of marrying her, have no doubt. It was such a surprise to her when I asked if she would return to the estate with all of the girls that I thought she would be overcome." Recalling how she had looked up at him – first with confusion and then with overwhelming joy, John felt his lips tug into a wide smile. "She is the most amazing young lady I have ever had the opportunity to meet, Alice. I know she will be the most wonderful wife."

Alice lifted one eyebrow. "And you shall have a brood of thirteen adopted daughters with you!"

That did make John catch his breath, but only for a moment. "I have everything in place. There are three governesses, the cook from the orphanage, a new host of maids and even a nurse to ensure that the youngest are well cared for."

A small, rather contented sigh escaped from Alice. "And you shall finally make use of all of those spare bedrooms in the east part of the estate, John." She smiled at him, her eyes sparkling. "All in all, my dear brother, I think you have done very well. You are a very different man from the man I returned to almost a year ago."

That made him smile, aware of just how much his sister had done for him. "You always had the very best intentions for me, did you not? And if you had not persisted in trying to help me, then I would still be struggling in the dark. *You* were the one who came to London and found Laura and Elouise in the first place. There is so much that I need to thank you for that I do not quite know where to begin or how to say it."

Alice reached over and pressed his hand. "You do not need to thank me, John. Seeing your happiness, seeing Elouise and Laura so wonderfully content is more than enough for me. Finally, I can think of my own future without any great concern for yours."

John regarded her curiously, his grin spreading across his face. "Does this mean, my dear sister, that you have finally chosen which gentleman's suit you will accept?"

Lifting one shoulder, Alice laughed and shook her head. "I'm afraid not, John, for they are both very charming. But fear not, the moment I do decide, you will be the very first to know." Her eyes brightened. "And you will be able to look into them for as long as you wish and as thoroughly as you wish before I accept their suit."

"I shall do just that," John replied, getting to his feet and bowing towards her, making her laugh. "And now, if you will excuse me, I think I hear a carriage approaching."

The moment Laura stepped into the hallway, John felt himself practically glow with happiness. She looked so delightfully happy, although her eyes were searching all over the place until, finally, she spotted him standing on the stairs.

"Royston," she breathed, holding her hands out to him. "Oh, Royston, I can hardly believe this! Here I am, finally, with all of my worldly things in the carriage...." She shook her head as he took her hands, her eyes still filled with astonishment as though she still could not take it in. "Is Elouise here?"

He nodded. "She is resting, I believe. She is quite worn out after all of her happiness with her friends."

"She was glad to see them," Laura murmured, not taking her eyes from him. "Just as I was glad to see her. I cannot believe that we are going to be together, *all* together, for the rest of our days."

John was about to say something more, but the butler appeared to take Laura's bonnet and gloves, asking if he could bring tea and refreshments for the lady. John, a little frustrated at the interruption said that they would be in the drawing room and led Laura away quickly, turning his head to catch the butler's eye and give him a stern shake of the head. He hoped the fellow understood that he was *not* to be disturbed for at least half an hour. He could not wait any longer before telling Laura everything he wanted in his future.

"Where is Lady Alice?" Laura asked as they entered the quiet room. "I thought she would be here."

Relieved that his sister had left the room – most likely to give him the time and the space required to speak to Laura with what was on his heart – he held Laura's delicate hand in his own, marveling at how soft and warm it was. There was so much he wanted to say to her, so much that he wanted to express and yet it was hard to find the words. His throat grew dry, his tongue sticking to the roof of his mouth as he took in her beautiful blue eyes, looking trustingly up at him as he turned to face her.

"Laura," he said, softly. "There is so much that I want to say to you and yet I find it difficult to put my thoughts into words. When I look back on the life I was living, lost in my grief and sorrow, I can barely recognize myself. Alice brought you and Elouise into my life – by force, I will admit," he said, with a quiet laugh, "but regardless it was your sharp words and refusal to allow me to treat you with disdain that forced me to reconsider things. That was the first shard of light into my life, I think."

Laura laughed softly, looking up at him. "I still remember how you came storming out of your quarters in such a furious rage at nothing more than a game of 'hide and go-seek'," she smiled, shaking her head at the memory. "You frightened me, although I may not have shown you that."

"You impressed me with your courage, your fortitude, and your strength," he murmured, gently stroking back an escaped tendril of hair. "And with your ability to beat me in chess – which I confess I still cannot believe!"

Her laughter lit up the room. "You could not believe it, as I recall."

"I still cannot believe it," he said, gently, lifting her chin with his finger. "My dear love, I cannot return to Royston manor without you by my side – as my betrothed."

Her smile faded from her face, her eyes widening and for a moment, John thought she might faint. Catching her deftly around the waist, he felt her step back slightly, but recovered herself, her fingers now wrapped tightly around his upper arms.

"What is it that you are asking me, Royston?" she whispered, her lips trembling as her face paled. "Are you...."

"I want you to be my wife, Laura," he replied, gently. "Say that you will be by my side every day of my life. Say that you will raise our *thirteen* daughters together," he laughed, as her cheeks brightened with color. "Say that you will bear our children and watch them grow, that you will spend your life with me at Royston manor, until the day we grow old."

Holding her tightly, John waited quietly for a moment as Laura drew in a deep breath, no longer looking as astonished as before. Instead, her lips curved into a smile, her eyes fixing on his.

"Oh, Royston," she replied, her voice hoarse and filled with emotion. "It is more than I ever dreamed of. Of course, yes, I will marry you. I will be your wife."

Slumping a little with relief, he held her close for a moment before seeking her lips, kissing her gently. She responded to him with more passion than he had ever experienced before, buoyed by the promise of a life together with him.

"Goodness!"

She stumbled back all of a sudden, one hand pressed to her mouth. For a horrible moment, John thought she meant to refuse him, thought that she meant to say she could not wed him – only to see her lips quirking from behind her hand.

"Oh, Royston, I shall be a duchess!" she exclaimed, having clearly only just recognized such a thing. "An orphaned girl to a duchess! How shall I ever fulfill everything that is expected of me?"

He reached for her and caught her hand, thinking to

himself that she would make the most wonderful duchess.

"My love," he replied, gently. "You will be a wonderful duchess and a wonderful mother to your girls – and to our own children, should we be blessed with them. You may know that I am not the most.....proper Duke, given my desire to have a house full of children and a complete disregard for what any of my neighbors and friends might think of my behavior – which is why I am quite sure that you will be a truly remarkable duchess. You are just the same as I. You care little for what people think and focus entirely on caring for those around you. You give more and more of yourself for the good of others and it is this that matters the most to me, Laura. Your generous nature, your kind heart, and gentle spirit are a treasure. Etiquette and expectation mean nothing, my love. You are already more than enough."

A single tear dropped to her cheek and he brushed it away with a gentle kiss, looking deeply into her eyes as she smiled up at him, clearly reassured.

"I want to give you the life you deserve, my love," he finished gently. "For you have already given me back my own."

"Then I will be your duchess, Royston," came her quiet whisper. "And you will have my heart for the rest of my days."

He made to kiss her, only for the door to fly open and Alice to burst inside, with Elouise by her side.

"Oh, we heard it all!" Alice exclaimed as Elouise threw her arms around Laura. "I am so very glad, so *very* glad!"

John laughed aloud as she embraced him, seeing Elouise looking up at Laura with shining eyes.

"You are to be my mother, then?" Elouise said, as Laura held her hands. "Truly?"

"Truly," Laura whispered, looking down at Elouise with sheer joy in her expression. "I *shall* be your mother, and Betty's mother, and Mary's mother, and Sarah's mother – in fact, mother to all of our dear girls. You shall be sisters, all of you, and we shall live happily together in Royston manor, as one family bound together with love, affection, and happiness."

Elouise sighed contentedly. "That sounds truly wonderful," she said, glancing back at John, her face a picture of happiness.

"Yes," he agreed, his heart full to the brim as he took in the scene before him. "And I think that is just what it will be."

CHAPTER NINETEEN

Laura looked up at John's smiling face as the carriages rolled up the gravel drive. They had already been at Royston manor for a day, having made exceptionally good time on their return journey, which had allowed them some time to ensure everything was in place for the girls. Sometimes, Laura had been forced to stop and pause in whatever task she'd been doing, hardly believing that this was truly to be her life. It felt like a dream at times, a dream she might wake up from at any minute and find herself back in Mary Sander's orphanage, doing her best to keep the girls fed, educated and happy. But now, finally, she was to have both her own dreams fulfilled, and that of the girls. They had what each of them had longed for – a home of their own, a home where they would be loved and cared for without any fear of being thrown aside – and she to live her life with the man she had come to love, the man who had become more to her than any other.

The Duke of Royston.

Even now, looking up at him, she could hardly believe that she was to be his wife and a duchess at that! When the realization had first hit her, she had been flabbergasted, thinking to herself that she would never be able to fulfil all that was expected of a duchess, but Royston had, in his own quiet and gentle way, put her mind at ease. The etiquette, the conversation, the manners and the expectations of a duchess would not be put on her shoulders. All he wanted from her was her love and her devotion, to both him and to the girls who she could now think of as her daughters. Love and devotion were the very things she wanted to give.

"Here they are," he said, reaching for her hand and holding it tightly as the girls waved at them from their carriages, broad smiles of excitement on every single face. "Our girls, my dear. Finally, they have come home."

The moment the carriages stopped, the girls practically fell from the doors, running towards Laura as fast as they could. She embraced them each in turn, hearing them all talking at once and laughing aloud at the joy that filled her. She could barely make out what anyone was saying and ended up picking Mary up, holding her on her hip as the child put her arms around her neck and held her tightly.

"You are quite safe, my darling girl," Laura breathed into her blonde hair. "Quite safe, I promise. You have done remarkably well."

"She did very well, miss," said one of the maids who had been accompanying the girls in the carriage. "Didn't fuss but the once, even though the drive was a long one."

Laura smiled and hugged Mary close. "Thank you. I

think the girls will all need to rest for a while before dinner. Come along, girls. Let me show you to your rooms."

Betty, the eldest stared at her for a moment, her eyes wide with astonishment.

"Whatever is the matter?" Laura asked, reaching for her hand. "Betty, are you quite all right?"

Betty's mouth open and shut and then opened again. "Do you mean, Miss Laura," she breathed, surprise written across her face. "Do you mean that we have our own bedrooms?"

Laura, realizing her surprise, smiled gently and pressed her hand tighter. "Oh, Betty. Your life is changing in so many ways. Yes, you have your own bedchamber, my dear, with a connecting door to Judith's room. The youngest will share a bedchamber and they have a nurse to take care of them. You shall have a life like you have never known before, my dear, and all because of the Duke's kindness to us all."

Betty wiped away a tear, turning to look up at the Duke. "Your – your grace," she stammered, clearly a little unsure how to address him. "Thank you ever so much."

The Duke smiled and put one hand on Laura's shoulder. "Betty, you are to call me 'Royston', just as Elouise does – or, and this is for all of you ." He waited until the girls had all stopped their chattering and had fixed their attention solely on him. "As I was saying to Betty, you may all refer to me as 'Royston' or, if you wish it, 'father' for that is what I intend to be to all of you. You are not to shy away from speaking to me, for I intend to be as good a father as I can be to you all, from the very oldest to the very youngest." Smiling, he ruffled Mary's hair before pressing a kiss to her cheek, making her giggle and turn into Laura's shoulder. "I know you have all lost those you love but, together, we can make one new family. Elouise, I am sure, has told you some of the things she has been up to whilst she was visiting here. I promise you that everything she has had, you are to have the same, if not more. Governesses will educate you and I myself will teach you how to ride. Together, we will all go on some memorable adventures that will fill our lives with happiness and contentment." His smile grew gentle as he looked across at his new family before his eyes caught Laura's, his hand gently squeezing her shoulder. "Before Elouise and Laura – I mean, Miss Smith – I was miserable, lonely and sad. I can tell you now that I am gladder than I think I have ever been. I am quite sure that, from this day on, our lives will be filled with happiness and joy, for that is what I feel this very moment, now that I am looking out at you all. My family. My girls. My life."

Such was the warmth in his voice and the happiness in his eyes that Laura leaned into him, feeling Mary grow heavier in her arms as her head rested on her shoulder. The child was falling asleep and, of course, she should be hurrying her inside so that she might rest in bed, but she did not want to break this wonderful moment. So, she lingered, seeing the beautiful faces of all of her girls looking back at them both with not even the slightest trace of fear or worry on their faces. Finally, they were free from the pain and grief that had held them for so long, no longer worried about what Mary Sanders would make them do, no longer weary from hours spent trying to earn their keep. Here was freedom, here was contentment, here was love. Together, just as Royston said, they would begin life together as one family, never to be separated.

Mary murmured something and shifted on her shoulder. Laura patted her gently, rubbing her back as the little girl fell back asleep. Looking up into John's face, she saw him smile tenderly down at them both before, in front of all the girls, he bent down and pressed a kiss to Laura's cheek.

There was an audible gasp of surprise and Laura felt heat rush into her face.

"I do have one further thing to say," the Duke continued, as the girls all looked at Laura in astonishment. "As you know, Miss Laura came with Elouise when she came to visit the Royston estate some months ago. I was not as welcoming as I ought to have been and Miss Laura made that very clear to me."

Laura shook her head, blushing furiously as the girls laughed at the Duke's grin.

"But," he continued, the mirth gone from his voice. "Miss Laura has become very dear to me since then. I asked her to stay along with Elouise, but she said she could not, because of the love she had for the rest of you."

Betty reached out and pressed Laura's arm for a moment, her eyes glistening with tears. "You have always taken such good care of us, Miss Laura."

The Duke slipped an arm around Laura's waist as Laura held Betty's gaze, smiling back at her. Her stomach began to fill with butterflies as her eyes flickered over the rest of the girls who were all listening to the Duke intently. How would they take the news that she was to marry the Duke?

"I am glad to say," Royston continued, gently, "that Miss Laura has agreed to marry me. She will be my wife, my duchess and, if you would allow her to be, your mother."

Laura felt every eye swivel towards her. She shifted Mary in her arms just a little, feeling heat creep up into her face as the girls gasped in astonishment and delight. Betty, who had been battling her emotions for some time, now burst into glad tears, doing her best to stifle them with her hands.

"Here," Laura murmured, carefully shifting Mary into the Duke's arms. Royston took the girl at once, his expression one of love as he cradled the sleeping toddler, who didn't so much as shift in her sleep as Royston took her in his arms.

"Betty," Laura murmured, reaching for her and holding her close. "Are you all right?"

Betty sniffed as more of the girls came to wrap their arms around Laura. She hugged as many of them as she could, seeing their shining eyes and excited smiles.

"I am just so very happy," Betty sniffed, wiping her eyes with her sleeve. "You are to be our mother, Laura, truly?"

"Truly," Laura replied, a warm glow of happiness settling within her. "If you will let me, of course."

Betty burst into fresh tears and threw her arms around Laura, holding her tightly for a good few moments. Laura held her close, knowing that, for a long time, Betty had longed for nothing more than a family she could call her own. Finally, she had it. They *all* had it, Laura included.

"You will be my bridesmaids, won't you?" Laura asked, as Betty wiped her eyes again and smiled through her tears. "It is going to be a very grand occasion and I must have as many beautiful bridesmaids as I can. I think thirteen bridesmaids should do it, what do you think?" She laughed as the girls began to talk all at once, their faces lighting up with excitement.

"Then I shall have to send for the seamstress," the Duke chuckled, coming to stand next to Laura. "For you are all to have new gowns but one that is made especially for the upcoming wedding, especially if you are to be bridesmaids!"

Laura looked up at him, suddenly anxious. "You do not mind, do you, Royston? I know thirteen bridesmaids is a lot but I thought – "

He leaned down and kissed her firmly, making the girls laugh and Laura blush.

"My love," he said, softly, looking deeply into her eyes. "I think it is a marvelous idea. In fact, I cannot think of anything better." He smiled at her and Laura let out a long breath of relief, leaning into him for a moment.

"Come along then," he called, as the girls stopped their chattering for a moment. "Time to go inside, I think. Let us welcome you to your new home!"

"*Our* new home," Laura whispered to herself, taking the hands of Sarah and Rosemary so they could walk together, as one family, into Royston manor.

CHAPTER TWENTY

John stood waiting for his bride. The congregation was already on their feet, the church filled with guests as they turned, as one, to look for the bride. The church looked beautiful, having been adorned with flowers and ribbons, but John barely noticed. All he wanted to see was his Laura walking towards him, ready to become his wife.

It had been three weeks since his daughters had made the long journey to Royston manor. They had settled in beautifully, and the sounds of their laughter echoing up and down the once empty hallways had brought a joy to his spirit. The governesses had arrived one week after the girls and, over the last fortnight, the house had fallen into something of a routine. In the morning, the girls would be taking their lessons, and, in the afternoon, they were often found running all over the estate. John did his best to ensure the bulk of his work was completed in the morning also, simply so that he could spend time with the children who had become so dear to him. Just as he had taught Elouise to ride, he had now begun to teach some of the others to ride – although some of the girls were much too afraid of the big creatures to go near them. He was having to encourage them slowly simply to pat the horses. Elouise and Laura had been a marvelous help in this matter and they had spent many an enjoyable afternoon together down at the stables. In the evenings, he had enjoyed Laura's company and conversation, although she had been quite caught up with all the little details of their wedding, which now, he was sure, he would come to appreciate.

His breath caught as the door opened and the music began to play. Little Mary came out first, being led by Betty who was dressed in her beautiful silk gown of light blue. They walked along the aisle towards John, who smiled at them both. Mary held a small silk cushion that held the ring that was to be placed on Laura's finger and, with a whisper of thanks and a light kiss to the girl's cheek, John took it from her. The two girls stepped to one side and, as John raised his eyes to the door again, he saw his bride approach.

She was more beautiful than he had ever seen her. A light veil flowed down over her face, but he could still see the way her eyes fixed to his. She was clad in a long, flowing gown of white, the train spilling out behind her as she walked. Long silk gloves were on her arms and the diamonds and pearls sewn into the pattern of her dress caught the light as she walked, making her almost sparkle with effervescent light. The bridesmaids came after her, their gowns the same color as Betty's, and on every face was the brightest, most joyful smile.

John held his arm out to Laura and, as she reached him, she looped her hand underneath and held onto him tightly.

He felt her trembling.

"You look beautiful, my love."

She looked at him from under the veil. "Thank you, Royston," she whispered, as they turned to face the priest.

It was such a wonderful moment that John felt as though he could not quite take it in. The vows were said, the sermon was delivered and then, being handed the quill and ink, John signed his name on the parish register. He watched as Laura signed her name also, before looking up at him with such a joy in her eyes that he felt almost as if he might weep with happiness. Carefully, he lifted the veil from her face as the congregation watched, wishing that he could press a kiss to her lips right at this very moment but knowing he could not for it was not right to do so within the church.

"I now pronounce you husband and wife," the priest finished, with a small smile. "May God bless you both as you begin your life together for His glory."

John took Laura's arm and walked with her down the church aisle, looking neither left nor right but directly at the door, as was expected. Once they got outside, however, and before the guests could appear to congratulate them, he pulled Laura into his arms and placed a firm kiss to her lips. There was so much he wanted to say to her but, for the moment, he could do nothing other than simply hold her as the glorious sunshine surrounded them both.

And then the doors opened again, and their daughters came out to join them, each chattering, laughing and smiling as they surrounded both John and Laura.

Alice joined them, holding little Mary in her arms. She kissed John on the cheek and them embraced Laura, tears shining in her eyes.

"I am so very glad for you both," she murmured, as Mary leaned in for Laura's embrace. "This is truly a wonderful day. Just look at you both! And look at your delightful children." She shook her head, clearly astonished at the way things had turned out. "I did not think I would ever be able to see you so free of the despondency that held you, John, but to see Laura standing by your side, with your daughters around you has made me happier than I ever dreamed. You are truly blessed, dear brother."

He smiled at his sister with Mary still in her arms, who was then borne away by Betty and some of the others, who were now all eagerly chattering about the wedding breakfast to come. John nodded and thanked the many guests who came out to offer them their congratulations, keeping one arm around his wife's waist.

"The carriage is waiting for us, my love," he murmured, leading Laura through the crowd of well-wishers, who threw rice as they passed. Laura laughed aloud as they half ran to the carriage, her joy evident.

He helped her up into the carriage and then climbed in himself, waving at the guests and at his daughters as they stood outside the church, waiting for them to depart. They would soon all arrive back at the Royston estate for the wedding breakfast but, for the moment, he had a few minutes alone with his new wife.

The carriage rolled away and he sighed happily, before pulling Laura over onto his lap. She laughed and settled into his arms, filling his heart as she did so.

"My Duchess," he murmured, looking down into her beautiful face. "My wonderful, beautiful wife. I do not think I have ever felt such happiness in my entire life."

Laura looked up at him, her face wreathed with smiles but with a single tear tracking down her cheek. "I love you, Royston."

His heart soared into the clouds. "And I love you, Laura," he murmured, lowering his head and kissing her with such gentleness and love that they both became quite lost, their hearts twining together as one.

I am glad they got their happy ever after!
Check out the next book in the series at the link below!
The Baron's Malady
Read ahead a few pages for a sneak peak!

MY DEAR READER

Thank you for reading and supporting my books! I hope this story brought you some escape from the real world into the always captivating Regency world. A good story, especially one with a happy ending, just brightens your day and makes you feel good! If you enjoyed the book, would you leave a review on Amazon? Reviews are always appreciated.

Below is a complete list of all my books! Why not click and see if one of them can keep you entertained for a few hours?

The Duke's Daughters Series
The Duke's Daughters: A Sweet Regency Romance Boxset
A Rogue for a Lady
My Restless Earl
Rescued by an Earl
In the Arms of an Earl
The Reluctant Marquess (Prequel)

A Smithfield Market Regency Romance
The Smithfield Market Romances: A Sweet Regency Romance Boxset
A Rogue's Flower

Saved by the Scoundrel
Mending the Duke
The Baron's Malady

The Returned Lords of Grosvenor Square
The Returned Lords of Grosvenor Square: A Regency Romance Boxset
The Waiting Bride
The Long Return
The Duke's Saving Grace
A New Home for the Duke

The Spinsters Guild
The Spinsters Guild: A Sweet Regency Romance Boxset
A New Beginning
The Disgraced Bride
A Gentleman's Revenge
A Foolish Wager
A Lord Undone

Convenient Arrangements
Convenient Arrangements: A Regency Romance Collection
A Broken Betrothal
In Search of Love
Wed in Disgrace
Betrayal and Lies
A Past to Forget
Engaged to a Friend

Landon House

Landon House: A Regency Romance Boxset
Mistaken for a Rake
A Selfish Heart
A Love Unbroken
A Christmas Match
A Most Suitable Bride
An Expectation of Love

Second Chance Regency Romance
Second Chance Regency Romance Boxset
Loving the Scarred Soldier
Second Chance for Love
A Family of her Own
A Spinster No More

Soldiers and Sweethearts
To Trust a Viscount
Whispers of the Heart
Dare to Love a Marquess
Healing the Earl
A Lady's Brave Heart

Ladies on their Own: Governesses and Companions
More Than a Companion
The Hidden Governess
The Companion and the Earl
More than a Governess
Protected by the Companion
A Wager with a Viscount

Christmas Stories

Love and Christmas Wishes: Three Regency Romance Novellas
A Family for Christmas
Mistletoe Magic: A Regency Romance
Heart, Homes & Holidays: A Sweet Romance Anthology

Happy Reading!

All my love,

Rose

A SNEAK PREVIEW OF THE BARON'S MALADY

CHAPTER ONE

Miss Josephine Noe, daughter to the late deceased Mr. and Mrs. Noe, sat quietly on a grubby step in Smithfield Market, trying her best to stop the cold wind from getting in through her moth-eaten shawl. Her unshod feet were raw with cold and she attempted to tuck them under her grubby skirts. Her eyes were red but there were no more tears left. She had nothing left within her to give. All she had to do now was survive.

The wind whipped about her and she shivered, trying her best to ignore the grumbling of her stomach. It had been hours since she'd last eaten and, even then, it had only been a half-rotten apple and a moldy bit of bread she'd found in an alleyway. There was nothing going spare and since she was only one of hundreds of beggars on the street, it wasn't likely she'd be able to survive if things carried on this way.

She'd thought to come to London from her home in Hampstead, hoping that she'd somehow find work and be able to scratch out a living, but that dream had died almost the moment she'd set foot in the city. There was nothing here but disease and death. The very same disease that had taken her parents and forced her from her village.

When her parents had become ill, she'd done everything she could to help them, but to no avail. What had made things all the worse was that she too had become sick but, for whatever reason, had managed to recover from it. She could still remember the ache in her throat, her pounding head, and skin that itched and burned. Her days had been filled with delirium until, finally, she'd emerged weak and frail, but no longer ill.

It had not been that way for her parents. Unable to do anything to help them, she had seen them taken from her one after the other. The agony of that still tore at her, bringing tears to her eyes whenever she so much as thought of it.

The village had not wanted her to linger, however. They had heard of this disease sweeping through nearby towns and had demanded that she leave the village for good, even though she had already had the disease and then recovered. There had been no other choice for her and she'd realized that it was fear that had forced her friends and neighbors to act as they did. Doing as they'd asked without protest, she'd taken the few things she had left and walked away from the only place she'd called home. The village folk had burned her parent's cottage to the ground, doing all they could to prevent the disease from spreading.

Josephine prayed that the village folk were safe. She

CHAPTER 1

was not angry with them for treating her as though she were some kind of leper, remembering how mothers had clutched their children to them as she had passed. Being in London these last weeks, she had seen just how truly awful this 'scarlet fever' was. The disease was terrifying in its swiftness, taking men, women, and children – although the children and the weak were often the ones doomed for death. Her heart twisted with pain and she rested her head on her knees for a moment. What was she to do now? Was she truly to have escaped death in Hampstead, only to face it again in London? If she did not eat, then she would soon be too weak to move and would end up being just another urchin dead on the streets of London.

Her body shuddered with the cold as the wind pierced her thin cotton dress, trying to make its way into her very soul. Hope was gone from her. She had nothing left in this world, nothing she could call her own. There was no-one to turn to, no-one whom she could go to for aid. Winter was coming and Josephine did not know what she was to do.

"Buy your bread 'ere!"

Her head shot up, hope running through her. The bread cart was passing by. People began to flock to it and, as Josephine watched, she saw a young beggar boy nip up to the cart. He was gone in a moment, a loaf of bread held tightly in his hand, his face lit up with a grin.

Josephine caught her breath. She did not want to steal, knowing that everyone was just trying to make a living of their own, but if she did not have something to eat then she would not last. She had to take what she could from where she could.

A shudder ran through her. The last time she had tried to take something from one of the market street sellers on Smithfield Market, she had almost been caught. Her hand had curled around an apple and thrust it into the pocket of her dress, just as a ruckus had started up only a few feet away from her. She could still remember the sight of it. A young boy, grubby, dirty and afraid, was screaming for his life. In his hand, he clasped something shiny, which she had known at once to be a coin. He'd obviously stolen it from someone and been caught and the terror in his face had burned into her soul. She could still remember how she'd backed away, her eyes fixed on the boy as a grown man had held him tightly. The constabulary had arrived, shouting loudly as they'd pushed their way through the crowd.

And then, the man holding the child had let out a scream of pain, taking his hand from the child as he twisted away. The boy had bitten him – a desperate act in order to get away. The constables had run immediately after him, their shouts of rage seeming to echo straight through her.

"Mark my words," she'd heard someone say. "It'll be the gaol for that young lad, if they catch him. He won't ever see the light of day again, I reckon."

"Let's hope they don't catch him then," said another man, with a wry smile on his face. "Poor beggar."

"Careful there!"

CHAPTER 1

The shout brought Josephine back to the present, back to her grumbling stomach and the ever-present fear of being caught. She could not be sent to gaol. The very thought sent terror straight through her, her heart quickening its pace at the fear of being thrown into some dark and dingy cell, with only rats for company. *He won't ever see the light of day again.*

Those words had her fixed to her step, despite the desperate urge to eat.

The man pulling the bread roll cart began to wave his arms as the people jostled about. A bread roll fell from the cart, landing on the cobbled street as the cart moved away.

Immediately, Josephine's eyes fixed on it. For a moment, her fear and her hunger battled against one another until, finally, she moved without hesitation. Dodging in between men and women, some with baskets and some who glared at her as though she were an annoying fly buzzing about their presence, she kept her gaze fixed on the small, dirty bread roll.

Her hands clasped about it with such gratitude that she almost felt like crying, but she knew she could not eat it here. Running back to where she had come from, she quickly sat down to eat, her teeth tearing off large chunks of bread as she grew desperate to satisfy the growl of her stomach.

Tears ran down her cheeks as she ate. This was not the life she was used to. Her father had been a laborer and her mother had taken in all manner of work in order to bring in a little extra money. She had helped her mother with the sewing and darning, with the herbs and remedies her mother had put together to help those who were sick, and what had been all the more wonderful was when she had been offered the chance to work as a maid at one of the great houses in Hampstead. It had brought a good wage with it, although she had been forced to improve herself in a good many ways even though she barely interacted with those in the house. The housekeeper had taken great pains to improve her speech, her posture, her manner of walking and her appearance. It had been difficult to be apart from her parents but it had been the chance to have a different life and, until the day she got word that her parents had become ill, she had enjoyed it. It was not a rich or abundant life, of course, but it was still a life where she had plenty to appreciate and enjoy. The money she had made working as a maid had been sent back to her parents for the most part, making sure that they never had to scrape about for food. They had never once had to consider stealing simply to satisfy their hunger. There had never been a lot, but there had always been enough. Now, even though she was alone on the London streets, she hated the thought of stealing but knew she would have to do so in order to survive.

She wiped away the tears with the back of her hand, leaving a grimy smudge on her cheek. Her fingers were red with cold but at least the roll brought a little contentment – not that it would last long. Closing her eyes, Josephine tried not to let doubts fill her. She had come to London in the hope of becoming a maid in one of the grand houses, but no-one would so much as look at her, not when she had nothing but the clothes on her back and no references of any sort. She would have had references, of course, had she not had to leave her position in the great house with barely a day's notice. But she had not been able to stay away, knowing that her parents needed her. So now, what was she to do? Was she to simply beg on the streets and pray to God that she would somehow make it through the winter? Was there nothing she could do?

"You there!"

Her breath caught and she forced herself to remain entirely still, frozen in place on her step.

"You! Girl!"

Slowly lifting her head, Josephine saw a tall, dark-haired gentleman moving towards her. He was wearing fine clothes, walking with the dignity and air of a gentleman. There was strength in his movement and, as he approached her, Josephine saw the slight lift of his chin and wrinkling of his nose, which betrayed his disinclination for the area surrounding Smithfield Market.

"Y-yes, my lord?" she stammered, wondering if she ought to stand but being a little unsure as to whether or not her legs would hold her up. "Can I help you?"

"Yes." He tossed her a coin which clattered to the ground. Josephine stared at it for a moment, before picking it up with cold fingers. She held it tightly in her palm, hardly daring to believe she had been given something so precious.

"Do you know your way about this place?"

Carefully, she got to her feet. "I do, my lord," she replied, hope bursting in her heart.

"I need to find a particular address and appear to

have become rather lost. I thought to walk, you see, since the day was fine," the gentleman replied, looking at her steadily. "You appear to be in need of some assistance also. If you are able to deliver me to where I need to go, then I shall be glad to recompense you in some way.

Josephine swallowed hard and nodded, the coin clutched tightly in her hand. He was to give her more, perhaps? More money meant that she would not have to struggle for food for some days, for the coin she had meant food for at least a week!

"I should be glad to help you, my lord," she replied, carefully, letting her gaze travel to his face and finding that there was now a small smile on his handsome face. In fact, he appeared to be quite at his ease and she found herself smiling back.

"Very good," he responded, grandly. "I am Baron Dunstable. I am charged with calling upon a family friend to take them to my estate for a prolonged visit." His expression changed. "The disease is taking hold of London and I must get her safe." Josephine noticed that his gaze had drifted away by this point and it was as if he were speaking to himself. She hesitated, waiting for him to say more, only for him to clear his throat and turn his attention back to her. Frowning, his brows burrowed down as he looked at her carefully. "You are not unwell, I hope?"

"Oh, no, my lord," Josephine replied, hastily. "That is, I have already had the fever and it has gone from me."

His expression cleared. "I see. You have recovered then?"

"Yes, my lord. A few weeks ago it was now."

CHAPTER 1

Nodding slowly, the gentleman studied her for another moment or two. "You speak very well for a...." He trailed off, clearly unwilling to call her what she was – a street urchin. She managed a small smile, hating her wretched appearance.

"I was a maid in a great house in Hampstead for a time," she said, by way of explanation. "The housekeeper there spent a lot of time working with me."

The explanation seemed to satisfy him. "I see," he murmured, his gaze a little interested. Stretching out his arm towards the pavement, his lips curved upwards into a small smile. "Then might we go, miss?"

A faint heat crept into her cheeks, embarrassed. "My lord, you have not said where you wish to go." She dropped her head only to hear him chuckle with exasperation.

"Indeed, I have not. It is not too far, I think." Quickly, he gave her the address and Josephine, relieved that she knew precisely where to go, began to hurry through the streets of Smithfield Market.

As they walked in silence, Josephine felt her despair begin to fall away. She would not have to worry about food or shelter for a time, if the gentleman was to be as generous as he promised. His funds would not give her any permanent solution, of course, not unless his fiancée's household was looking for a chamber maid, but at least it would take the fear from her back for a time.

"Have you no work?"

She turned her head, a little astonished that the gentleman would consider speaking to someone as lowly as she. "I – I cannot find any, my lord," she stammered, feeling heat rise in her face as she tried her best to speak properly. "I came from Hampstead to find work here but none would take me."

"From Hampstead, you say," he replied, easily, as they walked past the Smithfield House for Girls. "Why did you come to London? Was there no work for you back home?"

"The fever took my parents." The words came from her lips with no emotion attached to them, although it tore her apart inwardly. So many had lost loved ones, so many felt the same pain and grief she endured. She was just another one left alone on the earth, lost, afraid and without hope. Silently, she wondered if the Baron, being of the nobility, had lost any of his dear ones to the fever. Surely not, given just how different his circumstances were from her own!

"I am very sorry to hear of your loss, miss," he murmured, as they turned the corner into another street. "That must have been very painful for you."

She nodded but said nothing. She could not. The ache in her chest was becoming too great.

"My father recently passed away," he continued, as though he were simply talking to a friend. "That is why I am to return to his estate, although I suppose it is to be my estate now." Sighing heavily, he came to stand beside her as she came to a stop at the end of the designated street. "Grief affects all of us, does it not? No matter our circumstances."

Josephine felt herself wondering about this gentleman. He appeared both kind and gracious, which was not what she had come to expect from those in the nobility.

CHAPTER 1

Most often, they simply rode or walked past people like her, ignoring them completely, whereas Baron Dunstable seemed to be rather interested in her.

"You must be careful," he was saying, as she gestured towards the house where his fiancée would be waiting for him. "A young lady like yourself could easily become the prey of those who have less than pleasant intentions."

She managed a small smile, aware of just how intense his blue eyes were when they lingered on her. A little ashamed of her ragged dress and grimy face, she dropped her gaze and nodded. "Thank you, my lord. You are most kind."

The gentleman smiled at her again, his eyes alight. "Very good, miss. Now here, take this and ensure that you spend it wisely." He placed some coins in her palm but she did not look at them, barely able to keep her breathing steady. This was more than she had ever dared hope for.

"I think you will be wise with them, however," he continued, with a broad smile. "Thank you for your excellent navigation through the streets of London. I am in your debt." He bowed towards her, as though she were some elegant lady, before turning on his heel and walking away.

Josephine remained precisely where she was for a good few minutes, watching him as he left. Her breathing was quickening as she felt the coins in her hand, her legs shaking just a little as she slowly unwrapped her fingers to look down at them.

She gasped. The gentleman had given her five sovereigns. Five full sovereigns. That was more than her parents had earned in a year! Her eyes filled with tears and she held her hand close to her chest, feeling the warm tears slip down her cheeks. There was more than just money here, there was a place to sleep, food to eat, warm tea to drink and revive her. It would give her the chance to find work without fearing where her next meal would come from. Baron Dunstable had not simply given her money, he had given her a life. She would not need to fear the winter, nor even the one after that if she was careful.

Pulling her ragged handkerchief from her pocket, she wrapped up the coins tightly and tied a knot, making sure they would not jingle for fear they might be stolen. "Bless you," she whispered, watching him through tear filled eyes. "Bless you, good sir. And thank you."

CHAPTER TWO

"Georgina, really. You need not fuss!"

Miss Georgina Wells, daughter to Viscount Armitage, frowned heavily at Gideon and continued to smooth and rearrange her skirts.

"Georgina, please," he said again, growing frustrated with her constant attempts to ensure her skirts had not a single wrinkle in them. "You will only have to do so again once we reach the estate, which will be very soon."

"Then it is all the more important that I am quite ready and prepared to meet your mother and dear sister again, is it not?" Georgina replied, primly. "Really, Dunstable, you are quite impossible sometimes! Can you not see that this is of the utmost importance, especially since it is my new gown?"

Gideon held his tongue with an effort, despite the fact that he wanted nothing more than to state there was nothing wrong with Georgina's skirts and that no, new dresses were not of the utmost importance. Looking out of the window at the familiar landscape, he tried to let the frustration pass from him. He had known Georgina for a good many years and had always known that she did not care for anything other than herself. It was to be expected, of course, given that she was a young lady of quality who had been brought up to preen and simper and delight in everything she did and everywhere she went – but of late, it was beginning to grate on him. Mayhap it was because he had finally realized that the death of his father meant that he now had sole charge of the estate and all that went with it. Mayhap it was because there was this terrible fever sweeping through London, taking so many to the grave with it. For whatever reason, Gideon found himself growing more and more irritated with his bride to be. He did not care about new gowns or the like and was surprised that Georgina appeared to put so much stock into what she wore or whether or not the gown was of the highest fashion. Did she not see all that was going on around her? Did she not see the sick, the fallen, the poor and the needy? It was all he had been aware of since coming to London some days ago.

Sighing to himself, Gideon fixed his gaze on the window and did not let himself listen to Georgina's continued complaints about his lack of consideration for her and her gown. They had been betrothed for a good many years, due to the desire of both Gideon's father and Georgina's father, but he had never felt anything particularly for her and, even though he had not asked her, Gideon did not think that Georgina had any particular affection for him. That being said, whilst he had never found her particularly engaging, she certainly was beautiful and did well to be every bit the elegant lady she was expected to be – although Gideon was quite sure she had not been this vapid when he had first left for India two years ago, at the behest of his father. Having holdings in India, Gideon's father had thought it would be good for his son to see for himself what things were like and Gideon had rather enjoyed his time there, managing and ordering things. To hear that his father was deathly ill, however, had brought his joy to an end and so he had taken the first passage he could back home. It had been too late, however, for he had missed the funeral itself by over a month. Now that their half mourning was completed, Gideon was finally able to step back into society just a little, which meant that Georgina could make a long-planned visit to the estate.

Except, he did not feel any particular joy at the prospect.

His mind drifted back to the young lady he had seen on the steps, the one who had helped him to find his way. He could still recall how she had looked up at him with wide green eyes, clearly astonished that he would stop to talk to her. At one point, she had moved back from him, as though fearing he would either strike her or drag her away and he had felt his heart break. There were so many beggar children, so many orphans and street urchins but there had been something about this young lady that had spoken to his heart. Whether or not it was because he was afraid that she might be taken advantage of, beaten or worse, he had given her more than he had intended in the hope that she would make as much use of it as she could.

He had not meant to become lost in Smithfield Market, of course. He had been in the center of London and had become more and more astonished at just how desolate it seemed to be. It had not been the London he remembered, for it was quiet with an almost oppressive air. There had not been hackneys ready to take him to wherever he needed to go. There had not been carriages filled with the *ton*, all laughing and smiling and desperate to be seen. The quietness of it had been all the more evidenced by the fact that this was only just the end of the Season, a time when there ought to be at least a few more balls and soirees – but there had been nothing of the sort. The fever had scared the wealthy away, back to their country estates where they prayed they would be safe.

That fear had begun to linger in his own heart. His feet had ached in his boots as he had turned this way and that, growing a little more desperate with every minute that had passed. Having thought to go to the townhouse of his fiancée's father, he had begun to pray that he would either find his way there or somehow manage to make his way back to his own townhouse but had not managed to do either. It was obvious that Smithfield Market was no place for a gentleman of the *ton*. Men and women had jostled him without any consideration, shooting either vengeful glances or interested, conniving looks as if wondering what they could take from him. If he were to be attacked, he had realized, there would be no-one to come to his aid. The air had grown thick and his heart had quickened with anxiety. Despite this, however, he had lifted his head high and continued on as best he could, all too aware that the streets of Smithfield Market were not exactly safe.

The fever was in Smithfield Market too, he was well aware of that. As he had walked, a woman near him had stopped to cough violently, which had forced a frisson of fear into his heart.

Seeing the young lady sitting on that step had jolted that fear from his bones. She did not look as though she were about to attack him or steal from him, for he could sense a desperation coming from her. Her eyes were red-rimmed as if she had been crying, her feet bare and hands red with cold - and his compassion for her had burst to life. It was clear that she was living from one day to the next, never quite sure where her food would come from – and so he had taken a chance. A chance that had paid off for them both.

The grime on her forehead, the way her dark hair had swept about her thin cheekbones – he could not forget her face. How different she was to Georgina, and yet how much more in need of his assistance than his fiancée. Georgina came from wealth. He had more than enough to live on quite comfortably and yet that young lady, who he was sure was almost the same age as Georgina, had nothing. Her parents were gone and she had no work to speak of. Even though she spoke well and clearly had been given a very basic education from the housekeeper where she had worked, the young lady had no employment. None would hire her, he was sure, not if they discovered that she had already had the fever. Everyone was afraid, even of someone who had been struck with it, only to survive. He had spoken to her more than he had first intended, finding his heart caught with sympathy for her and aware of just how grateful she had been to him for what, for him, was a simple kindness. He prayed that she would not fritter away the coins he had given her, but that she would use it to find food and shelter for herself. He had wanted to do more, had wanted to demand that Georgina ensure the girl had a position as a maid or some such thing in her father's household but had known he could not do so. He would have sent her to his own townhouse, was it not shut up and empty of servants, for he had sent them all to his country estate to clean it from top to bottom before preparing it for his mother and sister.

That was not a conversation he was looking forward to having.

His mother, widowed and sad, would have to face the difficult reality that she would now be expected to vacate her own home in order to reside in the smaller estate Gideon had called his own for so many years. It was not something Gideon would push upon her, of course, particularly not when she was still grieving, but he had very little intention of bringing Georgina to live with him as his wife, only for his mother to reside there also. As for his sister, not yet out, he hoped that she would soon find herself a suitable husband or that she would be willing to consider relocating also. Again, it was not something Gideon expected to demand of her but it would be put to her gently, reminding her that a good many things were now to change. He was to be wed in a few months' time, once the banns were called, and would have to ensure that his new home was ready and waiting for them both.

It would be strange, of course, to now seat himself in his father's study, where he had so many fond memories of spending time with the good gentleman. His father had never been outwardly expressive with his emotions but Gideon had always known that his father loved him very deeply. He had done all he could to prepare Gideon to take on the title when the time came, and Gideon's deepest regret was not being by his father's side when he had taken his last few breaths.

"I do hope the fever has not reached here," Georgina said, breaking the silence that had fallen between them. "After all, part of the reason we are coming here is to remove ourselves from that *dreadful* city."

Gideon gave her a tight smile. "I do hope not, "he replied, realizing that, yet again, Georgina was displaying her inability to consider anyone but herself. "There has been a good deal of suffering already and one can only hope that it will come to an end very soon."

Georgina sniffed delicately. "I must keep myself as far away from those who are ill, of course. Father would be in such a terrible state of distress if he were to hear news that I was ill."

Georgina's father was to return from London to his country seat, whilst Francis escorted Georgina and her lady's maid to his own estate for a prolonged stay. "I am quite sure you can write to reassure him almost the moment you are received," Gideon replied, with a little harshness to his tone. "All will be well, Georgina. I am quite sure of it."

What happens with Baron Dunstable, Georgina, and Josephine? How does the scarlet fever epidemic affect their lives? Check out the full version of the story on the Kindle store The Baron's Malady

JOIN MY MAILING LIST

Sign up for my newsletter to stay up to date on new releases, contests, giveaways, freebies, and deals!

Free book with signup!

Facebook Giveaways! Books and Amazon gift cards! Join me on Facebook: https://www.facebook.com/rosepearsonauthor

Website: www.RosePearsonAuthor.com

Follow me on Goodreads: Author Page

You can also follow me on Bookbub! Click on the picture below – see the Follow button?

JOIN MY MAILING LIST

Printed in Dunstable, United Kingdom